NUTS AT CHRISTMAS

THE SHOOTING STARS SERIES

SIMON NORTHOUSE

FLABBERGASTED
PUBLISHING

For information about special discounts available for bulk purchases, sales promotions, fund-raising and educational needs contact simon@simonnorthouse.com or visit the Author's website at https://www.subscribepage.com/author_simon_northouse_home or Facebook page https://www.facebook.com/simonnorthouse

Published by Flabbergasted Publishing

First Edition

Kindle e-book ISBN-13: 978-0-6487619-8-3

Paperback ISBN-13: 978-0-6487619-9-0

CONTENTS

1: The First Noel

My wife has just dropped the bombshell and I've become collateral damage. I think the military term it, "caught in friendly fire." I'm annoyed, aggravated, displeased, and bloody narked—to say the least.

'Fiona, I wish you'd consult with me before you go making such big decisions,' I cry bitterly.

'I did. Your problem is you don't listen,' she replies in a carefree, happy-go-lucky manner which only adds to my displeasure.

'No, you didn't! I'm sure I would have remembered if you had.'

'Yes, I did.'

'When? Go on then, when exactly did you tell me?' She resumes hanging Christmas cards on a ribbon which straddles the fireplace.

'A couple of weeks ago. You were sitting in that very chair, watching the football. I said to you, "Wouldn't it be nice if we could get the band, their spouses and kids to spend Christmas with us." And you agreed.' I scrunch my nose up and try to recall this momentous event.

'Who was playing?'

'What?' she says, as she rearranges the cards on the ribbon.

'The football; who was playing?'

'Oh, I don't know. One team was in red the other in pale blue.'

'Hmm… it was a good game. Man City against Man Utd.'

'Yes, that was it.'

'And what was my response? Because I definitely don't recall you posing such an ominous question.'

'You said, "uh, huh". Which in my language means, yes.'

'Uh, huh, does not mean yes! It means I'm busy concentrating on the soccer and please don't talk to me until the final whistle has blown.'

'I took it as a yes. Anyway, it's too late now. I spoke to Jackie, Fiona and Julie last week and they think it's a wonderful idea. It's all been arranged. We'll have a ball.' I let out an expulsion of air and slump back into my chair. She glances at me over her shoulder, then comes and sits on my knee.

'Cheer up Mr Grinch. It will be fun.'

'No, it won't. It will be bloody hard work.'

'I just thought that with the older boys spending Christmas at my mum's it will be too quiet. Christmas is supposed to be a time for laughter, sharing, good company.'

'That's exactly what I was looking forward to—a quiet Christmas with you, me and Mary. Lazy days and walks in the Dales. Sitting in front of the open fire on a night and watching Christmas films together. Now it will be chaos and calamity. Non-stop cooking and cleaning and no one will be able to agree what we should do or where we should go.' She runs her long slender fingers through my hair.

'Don't be silly. Everyone will pitch in and I've already explained to them that each family can come and go as they please. They can do whatever they want. We're not all joined at the hip, you know. Think of the little kids, five of them running around the house, excited and giddy. It will be wonderful, a Christmas to remember.'

'You've got a strange idea of wonderful. As for it being a Christmas to remember, you're correct on that one, but for all the wrong reasons. One of those idiots is bound to do something stupid.'

'Who? The kids?'

2

'No, they're the least of my worries. I'm talking about Geordie, Robbo and Flaky.'

'Don't talk about your friends like that. I'm sure everyone will be on their best behaviour.'

'Geordie doesn't know the meaning of the phrase.'

'Hey, come on, be fair. Even you have to admit he's calmed down since he had those therapy sessions. He's like a new man.'

'Hmm… you don't know him like I do. He's a dormant volcano. It's not a case of *if* he erupts, it's a case of *when* he erupts.' She stands and heads towards the door.

'Okay. I'll ring everyone and cancel. It's short notice and I'm sure they'll be disappointed, but there's no point going ahead if it's going to make you miserable.' She heads out of the door.

'Wait!' I yell. Her head pops back into the room.

'Yes?' she asks casually.

'All right. They can come. But I'm warning you, when it all turns pear shaped, on your head be it. I'll definitely be using the phrase, "I told you so". I suppose they'll be arriving Christmas Eve and leaving Boxing Day. I guess I can put up with them for a couple of days.' I say, resigned to my fate. She avoids my gaze as she winces and clenches her teeth together.

'Hmm… well,' she says, tapping her lips with a finger.

'Fiona? What is it? There's something you're not telling me.'

'Ahem, they're here for the week. Arriving the day before Christmas Eve,' she mumbles, slipping into a whisper so low it's barely audible.

'Did you say a week?' She nods her head and pulls her "forgive me" expression.

'Oh, God… what have I done to deserve this,' I moan, thoroughly dejected at the thought.

'Hey, I tell you what, we have half an hour before Mary gets dropped off. How about we head to the bedroom? That will cheer you up.'

'Uh, huh,' I murmur, distracted by unwelcome thoughts as a black Christmas farce plays out in my head.

'Does that mean, "don't bother me until the final whistle goes" or does it mean yes?'

'It means yes.' She pulls me to my feet and leads me up the stairs.

'Oh, one more thing. The day they all leave is the day your mother and my mother arrive. They'll be celebrating New Year with us—for a week.' *Just shoot me!*

2: I Saw Three Ships Come Sailing In

I glance at the alarm clock—it's just after 7 am and the house is silent. It's the best time of day; peace and tranquillity. I throw my clothes on and slip into my shoes before creeping down the stairs. Caesar is already waiting for me in the hallway.

'How are you are going, old pal?' I say, as he sticks his snout into my hand. I scratch him on the head, then give him a lusty slap or two on his rump. 'Ready for brekky?' his ears dart upwards as he paces back and forth excitedly. I flip the kettle on and feed Caesar his breakfast, which he finishes before I've even dropped a teaspoon of coffee into my cup.

I pull the roller blinds up from the kitchen window and can't believe my eyes. The weather forecast had predicted a light scattering of snow and a frost but what lies in front of me is definitely not a scattering. It sits thick and deep. Branches droop from trees, burdened with a heavy white overcoat. Drystone walls have grown in height, now capped with at least six inches of icing.

'Wow!' is all I can say. I pour my coffee and make my way to the back door and creep out into the garden, followed by Caesar. He seems befuddled for a second before sticking his snout into the snow. He jumps backwards, lifts his head and sneezes. A moment later he gallops off into the garden to roll around in powdery drifts.

Every object, no matter how near or distant, is bathed in pure white. The only contrast is the sky, which is a stolid, dull grey, heavy with intent. It's cold; a brittle cold that can cut through clothes and gnaw at your bones. Thankfully, there's not a breath of wind. A perfect hush smothers the landscape, not even the call of a bird. I'm glad everyone arrived safely yesterday. If they'd made the trip today, they may not have made it.

I pull up a chair at the table, light a cigarette, then sip on my coffee and enjoy the serenity.

I drain the last dregs from my cup and head back inside. Muted voices emanate from the top of the stairs. I peer up to see three angels standing before me—beautiful, pure, innocent. Mary, Sally and Katrina smile back at me.

'Daddy, what day is it?' asks Mary.

'It's Christmas Eve, sweetpea.'

'I told you so,' says Sally, affecting a pout.

'Uncle Will?'

'Yes, Katrina?'

'Does Santa come tonight or tomorrow?' They carefully descend the stairs, holding each other's hands for support.

'He comes tonight, but very, very late, when little girls and boys are tucked up in bed fast asleep.

'We're not little girls!' remarks Mary, affronted at my description. 'We're big girls! We're five, five and five,' she says pointing at herself then her friends.

'I do beg your pardon. I didn't mean to insult you. Hey girls, I've something to show you that will knock your socks off.' I lead them to the back door and fling it open.

'Cool!' they all say.

'Guess what we're going to do this morning?'

'No, what?' says Mary.

'We're going to build a snowman!' They cheer and run around in mad little circles. 'But first, it's porridge for breakfast then you must get wrapped up in really warm clothes and put your wellies on.'

'But I don't like porridge. I think I'll have tomato soup instead,' says Sally.

'You can't have tomato soup for breakfast,' exclaims Katrina, who appears shocked at the very suggestion. There's a rumble of feet on the stairs. We all turn around to witness Geordie's boys come hurtling down, each clutching a giant water pistol. They're giggling but they're also fleeing. They jump the last three stairs.

'Hey, boys, what...' My words dry up as two powerful jets of cold water hit me in the face. They dash past and run outside, even though they're still in their pyjamas. A few seconds later Geordie appears at the top of the stairs wearing only a pair of baggy underpants. His hair is drenched, and he's red in the face.

'Are those two little buggers down there?' he demands.

'Yes, they just blasted me. They're outside.'

'Right, wait until I get my hands on them.' He clatters downstairs and races into the back garden. The girls and I are bemused at the scene. A seven-year-old and a five-year-old being chased by a near naked forty-year-old man who keeps falling into deep drifts of snow.

'Boys,' says Mary with a huff.

'Why are they always so silly?' Katrina asks.

'My mummy says they can't help it. It's the way they're wired,' offers Sally.

'Maybe they'll change when they get older,' Mary suggests.

'I don't think so,' says Sally, looking wistful. 'Look at Uncle Geordie running around in the snow in his underwear.' They all giggle. 'Let's get breakfast. Then we can build that snowman.'

It's nearing 11 am and the four husbands and kids have spent two hours outside building a snowman and an igloo. Everyone is chilled to the bone as we usher the children inside. Within minutes the house becomes a ball of confusion. There's constant noise in the form of excited chatter, laughter, tears, lectures, reprimands, threats and bribery. Drinks are spilt, food slides from plates, and there's bickering between the children about which Christmas film they should watch. After a fierce negotiation between the girls and boys, they compromise and settle on watching The Grinch as they take up their positions in front of the telly. I throw some logs on the fire and give it a stoke. At last, peace descends as the film begins. I hope it's not the calm before the storm.

I try to enter the kitchen to make a cup of tea, but it's like Piccadilly Circus in rush hour. The kitchen was commandeered by the women not long after breakfast, and they've been in there ever since. There is an onrush of last-minute cooking and baking.

'Excuse me, Fiona, I want to get in to make myself a cuppa,' I say in a pleasant voice.

'You'll have to wait! Can't you see we're busy?'

'How long are you going to be?'

'At least another three hours.'

'Christ! You've been baking for the last four days. There's enough food to feed an army.'

'It's to last all week. Once we've finished, we can relax and put our feet up.'

'What are you making?'

'I'm making a snowball cake. Jackie's making mince pies. Gillian is making a plum pudding and rum sauce. And Julie is… Julie, what are you doing?'

'Oh, I'm making a croquembouche,' replies Julie, who has flour over her face.

'A what bush?' I ask, perplexed.

'Never mind!' snaps Fiona. 'Are you going to get the damned Christmas Tree? I've been asking you for over a week.'

'It's tradition to get the Christmas tree on Christmas Eve,' I reply, nervously.

'In case it's escaped your attention, it *is* Christmas Eve! By the time you pull your finger out, it'll be Easter.'

'I was waiting until the kids finished the film, then I was going to get it.'

'No! Don't even think about taking the children with you. They're hyped up enough already. I know what they're like once the men take them anywhere; they come back sugared up and out of control. Why don't you, Geordie, Robbo and Flaky get the tree together? Get out from under our feet. What do you say, girls?' The other three women lustily agree.

'All right calm down. I'll round the boys up and we'll get the blasted tree,' I reply, grumpily. 'Jeez, all I came in for was a cup of tea and I get my bloody ears burnt off,' I mutter under my breath.

I enter the dining room and survey the scene. Geordie is at the head of the table cracking nuts. Robbo is to his right with his bare foot on the table clipping his toenails. Opposite him is Flaky, studying a crossword. *Do I really want to take these three with me to get the tree? I could slip away quietly and have a couple of hours peace and quiet, maybe one or two pints once I've bought a tree.*

'It's funny,' Geordie begins, 'I only eat nuts at Christmas. For fifty-one weeks of the year I don't go near a nut, apart from peanuts. Then Christmas comes along, and I eat nuts for a week.'

'Peanuts aren't nuts—they're legumes; from the same family as peas and lentils,' Flaky says as he lifts his head from the paper and stares at

Robbo with utter disdain. 'Do you have to cut your toenails at the dining room table? What's wrong with the bathroom?'

'The light's better down here. I can see what I'm doing.' Geordie munches on a hazelnut then washes it down with a swig of tea.

'Could you crack me a walnut?' Flaky asks, turning his attention to Geordie.

'You're missing a little word.'

'Please.'

'That's better. Manners cost nothing.' Geordie reaches for the bowl of nuts and picks up a generous sized walnut. 'Look at the size of that bugger!' he says with obvious glee. 'Walnuts always remind me of brains.'

'In your case, a scale model,' Robbo murmurs as he positions the clippers around his big toenail, an ugly yellowish specimen that looks like it belongs to a much older man. There's a click as the jaws of the clippers perform their duty, despite all the odds. The errant toenail spins silently through the air and lands without a sound in Geordie's cup of tea. Robbo swivels his eyes and peers into the cup. Geordie is still struggling with the walnut, oblivious to the foreign body that just swan-dived into his brew and Flaky has fixed his attention back on the crossword. Robbo furtively glances at me with one arched eyebrow.

'This cryptic is bloody tough today,' mutters Flaky. '10 across, 8 letters – "rodent goes crazy." What does that mean?' Geordie is going red in the face as he squeezes the nutcrackers with all his might.

' Squirrel,' I say. Flaky looks at me.

'Squirrel?'

'Yes… rodent goes crazy. Squirrel, nuts.'

'Ah, yes, of course,' he replies as he picks up his pen.

'Aargh, you stubborn little bastard,' Geordie says through gritted teeth, his whole body now shaking with the effort.

'That's a tough nut to crack,' Robbo mutters. The walnut has had enough of the unwarranted violence, and just when it appears that Geordie's head is about to explode, it departs from the nutcrackers at the speed of a sniper bullet. In the blink of an eye it traverses the short distance from Geordie to Flaky, hitting him squarely in the side of the throat, nearly dislocating him from his chair.

'You great big blithering idiot!' Flaky yells, rubbing his neck.

'Don't blame me! I couldn't help it. You crack your own bloody nuts, next time!' Geordie shouts back as he picks up his tea and takes a gulp. It takes only a second before a geyser of tea spews forth from his mouth showering Robbo.

'You disgusting, filthy cocksmoker!' Robbo bellows.

'He's a bloody liability!' Flaky yells. Geordie stares down at the pool of tea on the table and pokes his finger into it. He's puzzled for a moment before a flicker of realisation hits him. He slowly raises his finger in the air. Stuck to the pad of his index finger is the disagreeable toenail.

'Oh, you've asked for it this time!' The ensuing three-way argument grows in intensity as I watch on in silence, rather like a UN Peacekeeper. There's plenty of words I've heard many times before… and some new ones. The battle at "Dining Room Table," is brought to an abrupt halt as Jackie bursts into the room.

'Boys, boys, boys! What the hell is all this commotion? All we can hear in the kitchen is effing and jeffing. I've told you all before not to use the "F" or "C" word when there are children around, or at any time for that matter!'

'He threw a walnut at me,' Flaky says looking sheepish.

'I didnae throw a walnut at you! It was an accident. Anyway, I could have choked to death on Robbo's mutated toenail. What a way to go!' Geordie thunders.

'Hey, don't blame me!' Robbo yells. Just when it looks like hostilities are about to resume, Jackie brings it to a close.

'STOP! I don't want to hear anymore! Now quit your petty bickering and make yourselves useful. You're worse than the kids.' She turns to me. 'I thought you were going to get the Christmas tree?'

'I am.'

'Well, make sure you take these three dunderheads with you. Good grief!' she says as she stomps out of the room. So much for slipping quietly away by myself.

'Come on, lads. It's time for the Christmas tree run,' I say, wearily.

'Thank God for that!' exclaims Geordie. 'This place is like a concentration camp with the four Obergruppenführers in there,' he nods towards the kitchen. 'I made myself a brew earlier and I was lucky to get out with my balls intact.'

'Yeah, I'm with you,' drawls Robbo. 'They go nuts at this time of year. I don't know what gets into them.'

'I must admit, Gillian has been slightly tetchy with me today, which is most unlike her. What about the children?' asks Flaky.

'I've been ordered to leave them behind, on the threat of a court martial. Come on, let's get going. I'm sure we'll be able to slip in a couple of pints on the sly while we're out.'

Geordie and Robbo grin. 'Now you're talking, Billy Boy.'

'I like your thinking, William,' agrees Robbo.

'I'm not sure it's a very sage idea, Will. It's barely past twelve o'clock.'

'Shut up, you great big tart! You can have a ginger beer. It is the festive season, after all,' says Geordie, grimacing at Flaky. We put our coats on, then try to navigate the kitchen. I reach to grab my car keys as I squeeze past Fiona.

'No! You can't take our car!' she snaps.

'Why not?'

'Don't you remember? Last night we transferred all the kids' presents from the shed into the backseats and boot of the car, away from prying eyes. I've already caught Geordie's boys snooping around in wardrobes and under beds.'

'Oh, yeah, I forgot.'

'Don't worry, we'll take the Range Rover,' says Geordie. 'It's four-wheel drive, so it will handle the snow a lot better than that crappy Mondeo of yours. You've got no class.' The last thing I want is to get into a car driven by Geordie, especially in these conditions, but I can't be bothered to argue. The four of us make our way to the front door, leaving the carnage of the kitchen behind.

'Oh, Will, Geordie, Robbo,' calls out Fiona.

'Yes?' we all reply.

'Don't even think about slinking off to the pub for a few quick ones. I know what you three are like. We've still a lot to do and you all need to be clearheaded. There'll be plenty of time for drinking from tomorrow onwards. Do I make myself clear?' I pull my best "hurt," look as I exchange glances with Robbo and Geordie.

'It never crossed my mind,' I say, the emotion welling in my voice.

'I'm rather wounded by your assessment of us, Fiona. What sort of loving fathers and husbands do you think we are?' says Geordie, sporting a pained expression.

'We know exactly what sort of fathers and husbands you are,' states Jackie. 'Hence the warning. Keep off the booze, otherwise there'll be trouble… big trouble.'

'Ladies, fear not. I shall make sure everyone toes the line,' says Flaky. 'You can rest assured that on my watch not a drop will pass their lips.'

'Thanks, Flaky,' Fiona says, offering him a warm smile. 'Thank God one of you has some sense.'

'Robbo, you keep off the wacky baccy—understand?' warns Julie.

'For your information, I haven't brought my stash with me. I thought I'd go cold turkey for a week. Stick that in your pipe and smoke it,' he replies in a supercilious manner.

'I'm glad to hear it,' is his wife's only response. I usher the boys out of the door and close it behind me. Three of us let out heavy sighs.

'I thought this was the season to be jolly. It's like being at bloody school,' Geordie grumbles.

'Give the girls a break,' says Flaky. 'They've been hard at it last night and this morning. Tomorrow they'll be different beasts.' I glance back through the kitchen window and notice that Julie has cracked open a bottle of white wine and is filling four glasses… generously.

'Hey, take a look at that,' I say. 'Bloody hypocrites!'

'Aye, well what's good for the goose is good for the gander,' says Geordie, defiantly as he fastens the buttons on his olive-green trench coat.

'You mean, what's good for the gander is good for the goose. The gander is the female… you need to spin it 180 for it to work,' explains Robbo.

'Thank you, David Attenborough,' Geordie moans. He does a double-take at Robbo. 'What the hell is that you're wearing?' he exclaims as Robbo's coat becomes the centre of attention.

'It's a heavy-duty gore tex parka? This will keep me warm in sub-zero temperatures. Unlike your knackered old trench coat.'

'It's very black and shiny, isn't it?' chuckles Geordie.

14

'So what?'

'Nothing, just commenting, that's all. Anyway, I'll have you know that 70% of the body's heat is lost through the head.' He shuffles in his pocket and pulls out a furry Russian style hat and places it on his massive melon.

'Or in your case, 80% of the heat,' I say. 'You look like a Russian prisoner of war. Are you really going to wear that? You're in rural Yorkshire now. People will think we've been invaded.' Geordie adjusts his tifter with obvious pride.

'This, my friend, is a Ushanka.'

'A wanker in a Ushanka,' chuckles Robbo. We slip and slide our way to Geordies car and scrape and push snow from the windscreen and rear glass before climbing inside. As he starts the engine, I offer a word of caution.

'Take it easy, okay? No speeding. The roads will be treacherous. We don't want any accidents.'

'Chill out. I'm the safest driver on the planet. Plus, it's four-wheel drive.'

'You keep saying that, but it doesn't make it infallible. It still needs to have purchase with the road.'

'Don't worry. We have plenty of weight in the back, in the form of Robbo, to keep the wheels on the tarmac.'

'Sod off,' Robbo mumbles, as the click of a lighter is followed by the unmistakeable aroma of weed.

'If you're going to smoke that in here, open the bloody window,' Geordie says, frowning at him in the rear-view mirror.

'I don't believe it,' Flaky says, in a shrill tone. 'You told Julie you were off it for the week. You liar!' Robbo winds the window down and takes a lusty toke on his joint.

'Listen, pencil neck, being a husband is like being a politician. You tell people what they want to hear then do whatever the hell you want. Julie's happy—I'm happy. It's a win win.'

'Pathetic,' Flaky says as the car moves forward.

The road to Whitstone village is long, steep and winding. I warn Geordie that before entering the village, the road has one last sharp dip and bend.

'Geordie, start slowing down, now. We're coming up to the dip in the road.'

'Aye, no problem.' He hits the brakes hard. The car slews across the road.

'Don't use the bloody brakes, you idiot! Use your gears to slow down!' I screech.

'It's an automatic, you clown! It doesn't have manual gears. I cannae control that.' The wheels stop rotating, unlike the car, which begins a mad 360-degree loop. It slides up the edge of an embankment and clatters into a drystone wall with a thump, toppling a few copings. It ricochets off the wall, and completes another pirouette before coming to rest in front of a farm gate. A flock of sheep peer idly at us through the bars of the gate.

'Nice one,' I say, glaring at Geordie, as the adrenalin surges through my body.

'Don't blame me! You should have warned me! Anyway, it's my car that's picked up the damage so what's your problem!' The problem is obvious to see but I bite my tongue.

'This is an inauspicious start to our trip,' comments Flaky, in his usual patronising manner.

'If you have nothing positive to say, keep your big gob shut!' Geordie shouts.

'If he follows that advice, he'd be mute for the rest of his life,' Robbo chuckles. We get out of the car and inspect the damage. There are two big dints in the passenger doors and scratches to the back wheel arch. Geordie seems unfazed by it all.

'Surface damage. The insurance will pay for it. Not to worry,' he adds, rather jauntily, as we clamber back into the vehicle.

We set off again and within a few hundred yards we enter the sleepy hamlet of Whitstone. I spy the Beaconsfield Arms up ahead, as does Geordie.

'What do you reckon, Billy Boy?'

'Yep, good idea. I could do with a swifty to calm the nerves. Just the one, mind.'

'Aye, just the one.'

'Why are you pulling over at the pub?' Flaky pipes up.

'To calm our nerves after that harrowing experience,' I reply.

'No! Absolutely not. We've only been going five minutes and you want to stop for a drink? Didn't you hear what the girls said?'

'Aye, we heard what they said, but we didn't actually agree to their unreasonable demands—did we?' he says, grinning at me.

'I did! Flaky yells.

'Well then, you keep off the beer,' Robbo adds.

'I made a commitment to our wives to keep you in check. I forbid you to enter that pub!' We all ignore him.

'All those in favour of a calming ale to ease the nerves, raise their arms and say, aye,' I proclaim. Three arms are raised to the sound of three ayes.

'This is completely…'

'Carried unanimously,' Geordie says in a commanding, officious manner.

*****

Three of us finish our pints, Flaky his orange squash, and return to the car.

'Where exactly are we heading to?' Robbo enquires.

'There's a nursery in Skipton,' I reply. 'It's normally a pleasant twenty-minute drive, but in these conditions, you can double that, and then some.' Everyone seems suitably relaxed after a full-bodied pint of Timothy Taylors, apart from Flaky, who already has the gob on.

There's idle chit chat as we slowly navigate snow encrusted roads.

'Hey,' I begin, 'what the hell is a crockenbush?'

Geordie turns to me, as he has an unnerving tendency to do whilst driving. 'Not sure. Is it "broken vagina" in German?'

'You fool,' says Flaky. 'It's pronounced croquembouche and it's a French desert made with pastry puffs filled with cream and stacked into a cone shape then drizzled with syrup. I'd have thought Mr MasterChef, Will Harding, would have known that?'

'I don't do desserts. I'm a savoury man.'

'More like unsavoury,' Flaky murmurs from the back.

'Ho, ho, ho! Flaky cracks a funny. Well done, mate! They're worth waiting for; once every leap year.'

We drive on with petty bickering and barbs flying until we reach Skipton. The town is heaving with last-minute shoppers but we eventually find a car park behind the main high street and alight.

'Hey, Will,' Robbo says, 'is there a jeweller in town?'

'Yeah, there's two on the high street. Turn right when we get to the end of this lane. Why?'

'I need to buy Julie a Christmas present.'

'Christmas Eve and he decides it's time to buy the trouble and strife her Chrimbo pressy,' Geordie scoffs.

'I like to keep it real. I'm an impulsive sort of guy,' Robbo says. We round the corner into the busy throng of shoppers.

'Where's this nursery?' Robbo asks.

'Up here on the left. The jewellers are a few shops further up on the right.' Geordie spots a toy shop across the road.

'Won't be a minute,' he says. 'I'm going to check the toy shop out. Wallace is into the police at the moment, much to my annoyance. I've got him a bobby's hat and a uniform, but I can't find a badge to go with it.' He's already halfway across the road. Robbo also departs, bobbing along up ahead.

'Is there a delicatessen in town? I'm after some vegan cheese?' asks Flaky.

'Yeah, cross here and head down that laneway over there,' I say pointing. Flaky now disappears. *Great, nothing like teamwork. It's left to muggins here to get the tree.*

I saunter into the nursery and become immediately aware at the lack of Christmas trees. There's an old guy sitting behind the counter.

'All right, mate. I'm after a Christmas tree, about five to six feet in height.' The man takes a sharp intake of breath—never a good sign.

'Sorry buddy, sold the last one yesterday.'

'Hmm, is there anywhere else in town that sells them?'

'Normally, yes. But they've sold out too.'

'Christ, they're popular this season.'

19

'There's a shortage. The plantation that supplies most of the North burnt down during the summer. I did hear on the grapevine that a guy was selling some at the back of Kirkgate Market in Leeds. But it was only a rumour.'

'Okay, thanks.' I wander back to the car. This will not go down well back at HQ.

I'm standing next to the Range Rover waiting for the others to drift back. After fifteen-minutes I spot the trio of morons ambling towards the vehicle. They appear animated. It seems they're having a heated discussion about something. I wonder what it could be about? World peace, global warming, space exploration? After all, they are deep thinkers. As we pile into the car, the argument intensifies.

'It can't be called cheese if it doesn't contain any dairy products,' Geordie yells.

'Of course, it can!'

'Am I right, Robbo?'

'He's right, Flaky. By its very nature, cheese is made from milk.'

'What about soy milk, almond milk, rice milk? Hmm? Those products don't contain dairy and they're called milk.'

'He has a point, Geordie,' Robbo says as he effortlessly changes positions.

'Bollocks! Those products take their name from the verb of milk, i.e. to extract a liquid.'

'That makes sense. You can't argue with that, Flaky,' Robbo says as he flips sides again.

'In that case vegan cheese takes its name from the verb of cheese, because it looks like cheese.'

'Yeah, good call,' Robbo says.

'Codswallop! There is no "verb" for cheese, you numpty!'

'Boys, boys, boys,' I intervene. 'As fascinating as this debate is about the etymology of the words "cheese and milk", we have a bigger problem to address.'

'Hey, where's the tree?' Geordie asks.

'Exactly. There are no trees. There's a shortage this year. Something to do with a fire during the summer,' I explain. I rub my neck and glance sideways out of the car window. My eyes rest on a welcoming sight. 'I suggest we retire to The Boars Head, over yonder, and discuss our predicament and put our collective heads together to find a solution. All those in favour raise their right hands and say aye.'

'No, absolutely not. That's not a solution, it's an excuse to…' Three arms are raised followed by three ayes.

'The ayes have it. Carried unanimously,' confirms Geordie.

*****

We're sitting around the table slowly quaffing our beer. Even Flaky has opted for a pint of bitter rather than his usual orange juice.

'The only option is to drive to Leeds,' Flaky says.

'It looks that way,' Geordie agrees. 'How long will it take, Bill?'

'About an hour under normal conditions. With all this snow around, it could take another half hour or more. That's before we hit the Christmas traffic on the ring roads. Then we have to find a parking spot. The place will be jam packed.'

'And there's no guarantee of a tree when we get there,' Robbo adds.

'That's right. We're probably looking at a round trip of over four hours on what could be a fool's errand,' I say.

'Looks like you're up shit creek without a paddle,' Geordie says. 'I wouldn't want to be in your shoes when you break the news to Fiona, especially since she's been telling you all week to get a tree.'

'He's right, Will,' Robbo says. 'Never put off today what you should have done tomorrow… no hang on, never put off tomorrow what…'

'Oh, button it, you buffoon. Hang on, I have an idea. There's a pine plantation up near Fallside Gap. It's about halfway between here and Whitstone. I know they logged part of it a couple of years ago, so there should be some new saplings ripe for the picking.'

'You mean, cut one down?' Flaky says wearing a frown.

'Yes. They won't miss one.'

'Is that illegal?'

'Technically, yes. Ethically and morally, no.'

'How do you work that one out?'

'Imagine the distraught faces of our children when we return without a tree.'

'Aye, not nearly as distraught as the look on Fiona's face,' Geordie scoffs. I ignore him and continue.

'They'll be heartbroken. The Grinch stole Christmas. Morally, it's our duty to cut down a tree.'

'You have twisted logic. I for one am dead set against it,' Flaky huffs.

'All those in favour raise their right arm and say aye.' Three arms are raised followed by three ayes.

'The ayes have it unanimously,' Geordie confirms.

'We'll need a saw or an axe,' I say. 'You don't have one in the back of your car, do you?'

'Of course I bloody well don't. Do I look like a serial killer?' says Geordie.

I study him. 'Yes. Not to worry. There's a hardware store on the high street, two doors up from the toy shop. Geordie, you nip back and get a saw.'

'Why me?'

'Because you know where the toy shop is.' He appears baffled for a moment.

'Aye, okay, I suppose so,' he eventually mumbles. I can't believe he fell for that one.

'Right, come on, sup up your beer and let's make tracks.'

*****

Geordie throws the saw into the boot of the car, then slams it shut.

'Robbo, what did you get the missus from the jewellers?' I ask as Geordie jumps into the driver's seat. Robbo leans forward and holds out a little ring box covered in black velvet with the words "Tiffany & Co" embossed on the lid.

'Take a look at this,' he says with pride. I open the box and pull out the ring.

'Wow! That's impressive. You're in for some serious brownie points with this. Are they real diamonds?'

'They sure are. Five carats.'

'Here let me have a look,' says Geordie. As quick as a flash Robbo leans over and snatches the ring back.

'Not on your nelly, mate! You'd probably drop it down a drain or something.'

'How much did that cost you, five carats is pretty expensive?' Flaky enquires.

'Five big ones,' Robbo smiles.

Geordie snorts. 'You paid five hundred quid for a bloody ring?'

'Nah, mate. I paid five grand for a bloody ring,' Robbo corrects. I fear Geordie's head is about to explode.

'You need your bumps feeling,' he chides.

'What did you get, Gillian?' I ask Flaky.

'A nice silver bracelet she's been eyeing up for some time. Not as exorbitant as Robbo's ring, though. But it still set me back £800. What did you get Fiona?'

'A coffee maker, a Gucci handbag and a £300 gift voucher for a fashion store.'

'Nice,' Robbo says.

'And a few special gifts for the bedroom,' I add. Robbo and Geordie grin.

'What sort of gifts?' asks Flaky. 'A scented candle or a bedside rug? That sort of thing?' Geordie and Robbo roll their eyes.

'Yeah, something like that,' I reply. 'Geordie, what did you get Mrs Kincaid?'

'A box of Milk Tray chocolates, a £50 Sportsgirl voucher and a new cover for the ironing board.'

'The last of the big spenders. You tight Scottish git!' I laugh.

'I'm not tight!' he argues.

'Face facts Geordie,' says Robbo, 'you're that tight your arse cheeks squeak when you walk.'

'Hey, who got the last round in? Me! Who's just spent £15 on a bloody saw? Me. Anyway, that's all she wanted. She specifically said not to get her anything expensive, she has everything she needs.' The three of us let out sighs and moans.

'How long have you been married?' Robbo asks.

'Coming up for seven years.'

'You should have learnt by now.'

'Learnt what?'

'When a woman says not to get her anything, that she has all she needs, what she's really saying is, "Listen shitface, you better get me something bloody good this year. I deserve it after putting up with you for the last twelve months." Jeez, Geordie, get with the program.'

'Robbo's right, Geordie. It's not what women say, it's what they don't say. Therein lies the path to a happy relationship,' I add.

'Listen, face-ache, me and Jackie have an implicit understanding of one another. We're like two peas in a pod. I can read her like a book. If she said not to get her anything expensive, then she meant it.' He starts the engine and reverses aggressively, swinging the car around and nearly cleaning up an old man on a mobility scooter. The guy toots his horn. Geordie winds the window down, sticks his noggin out and yells at him.

'Hey, pal, watch where you're going! It was my right of way. You're going to cause an accident if you keep driving like that. Lucky for you I have lightning fast reflexes, otherwise we'd be scraping you up off the road!'

3: Oh, Christmas Tree

We're heading towards the plantation along winding country roads, flanked by bare native trees and high stone walls.

'How much further?' Geordie asks.

'Not far. Just around the next bend.' The car slows as we navigate a tight corner. 'We're here. Pine trees dead ahead. There's a gate up on the left. Drive past it a little way and we'll park up. No point leaving the car where everyone can see it.'

'Those are big bloody pine trees, Will,' Robbo says.

'Yes, they are. There'll be a new patch somewhere with trees the right height. It's a matter of finding them.' We drive past the entrance and round another bend in the road before parking in a small layby. We jump out of the car, fasten our coats, pull our gloves on and adjust the scarves around our necks. Geordie goes to the boot and retrieves the saw. I'm bemused to say the least and realise I should have gone to the hardware store myself.

'What is that?' I demand, pointing at the saw.

'This, my little Yorkshire Terrier, is a 26-inch Spear and Jackson hand saw.' He holds it aloft as though he's brandishing Excalibur.

'You bloody idiot! That's no good for cutting a tree down. The teeth are too fine. I meant for you to get a tree saw, you know the curved type, with coarse teeth! It will take all day to cut through a trunk with that thing,' I shout.

'You never said that did you? There's no pleasing you sometimes!' he returns fire. 'Anyway, believe me, this will do the job. They don't make them like this anymore.'

'Obviously they do, considering you've just bought one. Come on, let's get going.' We hurry towards the entrance to the plantation. Stone walls, about chest height, sit either side of a large farm gate which is secured with a chain and padlock. Geordie hands me the saw as he inspects the gate. A sign, mounted on two wooden poles, protrudes from behind the left-hand wall. Flaky stands before it and reads aloud.

'Private property. Trespassers *will* be prosecuted. Cumberfutch Estates. And you'll notice the word "will" is italicised. That's that then, we definitely can't go in otherwise we'll be trespassing. I'm not willing to break the law.' He pulls his gloves off and doubles over to tie his shoelace.

'Here, hand me that,' says Geordie. I pass him the saw. He sidles up behind Flaky, bends the saw almost double then releases it. A satisfying "thwack" breaks the silence as the blade of the saw thumps into Flaky's buttocks. He lets out a piercing yelp as he hops forward like a frog on a hotplate.

'You great big stupid Jabberwocky! What the hell did you do that for?' he screeches.

'Because I had an overwhelming desire to do so,' says Geordie. 'That's what you get for being a quitter. It's always the same with you—the first hurdle we hit and you're ready to throw the towel in. You'll get nowhere in life with that attitude.'

'Don't talk to me about attitude! You have the worst attitude I've ever come across. You have scant regard for the laws of the land.'

'Laws are made by men and they're meant to be broken. If we didn't break laws, we'd still be sending five-year-old kids up chimneys and women wouldn't be able to vote.'

'Read the sign, stupid! It's there in black and white; trespassers *will* be prosecuted!' Geordie walks to the sign and begins sawing at one of the

27

poles. It only takes a dozen or so powerful thrusts, and he cuts through it. He starts on the second pole and within seconds the saw rips through that one too. The sign falls silently into the thick snow. Geordie picks it up and tosses it over the wall.

'Sign, I don't see a sign. Do you see a sign, Robbo?'

'Nah, mate. I can't see a sign.'

'Bill, can you see a sign?'

'Not anymore.'

'I think your eyesight may be failing you, Flaky. There's no sign here. Right, come on, let's get this tree.' Flaky is not appeased. I'm not sure whether the steam rising from him is coming from his mouth or from his ears. He rubs vigorously at his left buttock, still smarting from the saw slap.

'Trespassing, damaging private property, vandalism, theft…'

'Oh, stop your blethering man,' says Geordie as he climbs the gate and leaps down to the other side. I follow suit as Robbo sparks up a spliff.

'For the record, I want to say that I will come along with you on this foolhardy expedition for the sake of cooperation. However, let it be noted that I am adamantly against this mission.'

'Oh, chill out, Flaky,' says Robbo as he languidly ambles over the gate. 'It's hardly the Great Train Robbery, is it? It's a small bloody tree.'

'Aye, and think about poor little Katrina's heartbroken face if daddy returns home without one,' chirps in Geordie. Flaky reluctantly scales the gate as we set off deep into the plantation.

We walk on for fifteen minutes, flanked by tall pine trees. Their close-knit canopy blots out the sky and there's an eerie silence that accompanies the dark shadows. We eventually burst out of our murky tunnel into a breath-taking panorama. In the distance is the unmistakable outline of Inglegor Pike. To our left, the tall pines abruptly stop, and a little way ahead is a new plantation of small saplings. To our right is Fallside

Gap, a huge, steep embankment that stretches on for miles. We stop to admire the beauty as large flakes of snow dance down from bruised clouds above.

'That is a sight to die for,' says Geordie, in awe.

'It's beautiful,' agrees Flaky.

'It's like we're the first people in the world to set foot here,' Robbo says. Geordie bends down and picks up a handful of snow and fashions it into a compact snowball. He then drops it back into the snow. He pushes it along with his boot, each rotation exponentially increasing the bulk of it until it's the size of a basketball.

'What are you going to do with that?' Robbo asks.

'I'll give you a clue,' he replies. Geordie stoops and lifts the giant snowball up, then slams it over Robbo's head. Robbo's body remains the same, but his head has quadrupled in size and lost any distinguishing features. Geordie walks back to me.

'I tell you what, Bill, Scotland is the most majestic place on earth, but Yorkshire is a close…' He doesn't get a chance to finish his sentence as a splat of snow hits him fairly and squarely in the mouth. I glance over at Flaky who is grinning as he busily compresses snow together ready to launch his next missile.

'Oh, you've asked for it now,' Geordie says with a mischievous leer before another snowball thumps into the back of his head, this time from Robbo.

'Snowball fight!' I yell as we scatter in different directions. I try to keep my distance from Geordie as I know what the big clod is like. He can take things too far, although what damage he could do, out here in the open, surrounded by soft snow, doesn't immediately spring to mind. The fight lasts about ten minutes until we are all sweating and panting.

'Okay, ceasefire! Ceasefire!' I yell, drawing in deep breaths of cold dry air that stings my throat. Geordie and Flaky drop their projectiles, both laughing like drains.

'Oh, that was fun,' Flaky says, between deep gasps.

'I haven't had a snowball fight in years. I think the last time was when…' once again, his sentence is brought to an abrupt halt as a ball of snow smacks him in the face. Robbo is about ten feet away, chuckling to himself.

'What a shot,' he says. Geordie purposefully wipes the snow from his eyes and coughs out some more. He grins at Robbo.

'You shouldnae have done that, little man.' Robbo spins on his heels and runs as fast as one can in deep snow. It doesn't take long for Geordie to catch up and bring him crashing down with an athletic rugby tackle. He stands up, grabs the bottom of Robbo's trouser leg with one hand and Robbo's wrist with the other, and spins him around and around like a hammer thrower. After several accelerating revolutions, he heaves the hapless Robbo into the air. The three of us gawp in amazement as he takes flight. Unfortunately, for Robbo, his trajectory has sent him onto the wrong side of Fallside Gap, the south side. He lands on his back and takes off at lightning speed down the hill.

'Shit the bed,' I whisper, 'Look at him go. He looks like an unmanned bobsleigh.'

'Nah, more like an upturned dung beetle skimming across glass,' Geordie counters.

'I think he's gathering speed, not slowing down,' I add.

'Aye, it is a steep hill,' Geordie comments, wryly.

'A very steep hill, and a very long hill,' Flaky says. 'He's bound to stop soon.'

'I hope so,' I say.

'Why?' asks Geordie.

'Because at the bottom of Fallside Gap is Fallside Beck.'

'Is it deep?'

'Nah. But it's very wet.' Robbo's now nothing more than a black blob in the distance. We watch in silence for another few seconds. 'I think he's stopped. He appears to be waving at us.'

'No,' Flaky says, 'he's cupping his hands together.' A distant shout drifts to us in fragments.

'What did he say?' Geordie asks.

'Not sure,' Flaky replies. 'But it was definitely expletive laden.' We flop down onto the cushion of snow and wait for the return of the abominable snowman.

*****

'No, Geordie, that's way too big. I'd have to smash a hole in the ceiling for that to fit in the living room,' I say staring at the tree.

'You've got high ceilings. I'm pretty sure it will fit.'

'Don't talk ridiculous,' Flaky says. 'By my estimation that tree would be nudging fifteen feet, maybe more.'

'He's right, Geordie. Will would have to remove the roof to accommodate that bugger,' Robbo says.

'Aye, but look at her, she's an absolute beauty. The shape, the bushiness, the deep rich greenery. She's a true queen amongst an unruly mob of peasants.' Apparently, the tree has now been sexed and crowned.

'It is a grand tree, Geordie, I'll give you that. But there's no point having a beautiful tree if it's too tall for the room,' I reason. Geordie circles the pine for about the tenth time, gently caressing the needles. I do believe he's in love.

'How about we mount it outside, near the porch in front of the living room window? It will look great with Christmas lights and real snow on it.'

'He has a point,' Robbo agrees as he lazily tokes on a joint. I turn to Flaky.

'What do you think?'

'Well...' The sound of frenzied sawing fills the air. 'I guess it will have to work, now. The moron has started sawing.' A few minutes go by as Geordie works like a madman at the base of the tree.

'Timber!' he shouts, as a splintering sound cracks out across the countryside. Everyone runs for cover as the mighty pine crashes into the snow.

The damn thing has some weight to it, and it takes the four of us, placed strategically along the trunk, to carry it. Despite its bulk we make excellent progress as we retrace our footsteps back through the dark pine tunnel towards the entrance. We spot the gate in the distance.

'Nearly there, boys!' Geordie calls out in a cheery tone.

'Have you thought how we're going to attach this to the car?' Flaky queries.

'Probably with great difficulty,' I reply.

'Nah, it will be a breeze,' says Geordie. 'A couple of ropes is all we need to strap it down. It's not far back to Will's gaff, anyway.' A loud click followed by a posh, authoritarian voice makes us stop dead in our tracks.

'Stop right where you are, drop the tree, put your hands in the air and turn around... slowly.' We obey the commands in silence. A smartly dressed older man, in riding boots, jodhpurs and a heavy fawn coloured sheepskin jacket, is sitting astride a magnificent chestnut mare. In his hands is a double-barrelled shotgun, aimed directly at us. I assume it's loaded.

'And who might you be?' Geordie asks, scowling at the imposition.

'I am Lord Cumberfutch, 10th Baron of Upper Cravensdale and this is my land, that is my tree, and you four reprobates are trespassing.' We share hangdog glances with each other. Flaky is the first to speak.

'It's like this, Lord Fumberclutch…'

'Cumberfutch,' he corrects, rather patiently.

'Ahem, the thing is we can't get a Christmas tree for love nor money. There's apparently a shortage and our young children will be extremely disappointed if we return home without one. So, we thought…'

'I don't give a damn about your children or your lame excuses. There's clear signage at the entrance to this plantation stating that trespassers *will* be prosecuted and that's exactly what I aim to do with you lot. Now start walking towards the gate and keep your arms raised.'

'You cannae argue with his type, Flaky. They think they own the place,' Geordie moans.

'I do own the place—all ten thousand hectares of it.'

'You see what I mean?' Geordie continues. 'How can one man possibly own so much land? It's ridiculous.'

'People think Britain is a democracy, but it's not really,' I begin. 'It's the same old feudal system that's been thriving for thousands of years. Carve the land up between a few kings, earls and dukes and even lowly barons, and the rest of us can go to hell.'

'Aye, bring on the revolution, I say,' Geordie sighs.

'Can you two shut up,' Flaky hisses. 'You're not helping the situation.' Geordie ignores him.

'I mean, who gave him this land? One of his ancestors probably saved some distant king from being gored to death by a wild boar while out hunting. Or maybe he gave the king a hand job every night while on the crusades, who knows? But he was rewarded handsomely with ten thousand hectares that previously belonged to the people.'

'Aha! Not only trespassers and thieves but also left-wing rabble rousing agitators. I'm going to enjoy prosecuting you lot. I'm sick to death of your type tramping over my property. I aim to make an example of you.' We arrive at the entrance. 'Right, turn around and back up towards the gate,' he orders. 'Keep your hands where I can see them.' He stares into the vacant space where an hour ago a sign used to stand. He spots the vandalised signage laying on top of some fallen branches. 'And another misdemeanour to add to the growing list—destruction of private property.'

'I told you so,' Flaky whispers from the corner of his mouth.

'And what makes you think it was us who cut your sign down?' says Geordie, clutching the 26-inch Spear and Jackson saw in his hand.

'Possibly the hand saw gives it away,' he replies.

'Purely circumstantial,' Robbo states, who seems to have a layman's knowledge of the law.

'You really are a bunch of outlaws, aren't you? In the olden days you would have been swinging from the gallows by now,' he says as he slips the shotgun into a holster attached to the horse and dismounts. 'Don't try any sudden moves. I can retrieve that gun faster than you can cover the ground.' His expression and tone of voice has been emotionless throughout. He's cold, matter-of-fact, almost weary and resigned. He pulls his mobile phone from his jacket and scrunches his face. 'Damn and blast,' he mumbles to himself.

'What's wrong your Holiness?' sneers Geordie. 'No signal?'

'Hmm, we'll have to do it the old-fashioned way.' He puts his phone away, then pulls out a tiny notepad and pencil from inside his jacket. He nods at me. 'Name?' he commands.

'John, John Lennon,' I reply. He licks the tip of his pencil and writes.

'And you?' he says, nodding at Geordie.

'Paul McCartney.'

'Paul Mc...Cart...ney,' he repeats slowly, purposefully.

'Next,' he says, glancing at Robbo.

'Harrison, George Harrison, first class bombardier, at your command—SIR!' The Lord throws him a look of disdain and shakes his head before licking his pencil again.

'George Harri... son...' He freezes. 'Oh, I see, degenerates and smartarses to boot. Don't think you can escape your fate. The long arm of the law is very long indeed.' He puts the pencil and notepad away and pulls out his phone again. He takes a snap of the fallen sign, the sawn-off posts, then aims his phone at the four of us. 'Smile for the birdy.' We all wave and smile.

'Cheese,' Robbo says, as there's a click from the phone.

'I'm sure the police will track you down based on your mugshots. You've probably got previous.'

'What happened to make you such a bitter and twisted old git?' Geordie scoffs. For a moment the Lord's deadpan expression changes. His eyes glaze over as he stares straight through us. He blinks and his vacant expression returns.

'Right, get out of my sight. The next time I see you lot will be in court where undoubtedly, you'll receive a hefty fine, as a minimum, hopefully a short prison term. Let me make you aware that I have many powerful and influential friends who can make life very difficult for you. I'd have thought men of your age would have known better. Now skedaddle you bunch of hooligans.' We quickly climb the gate and head back down the road towards the car.

'How come whenever I'm with you lot I find myself in hot water?' Flaky says.

'Stop your quibbling, you big Jesse!' Geordie says.

35

We climb into the car and double back on ourselves. As we pass the gate to the plantation, we witness the distant figure of his Lordship trotting back towards Fallside Gap.

'There's only one thing for it, we must head to Leeds and hope they have some trees at the market,' Flaky says.

'No way,' I begin. 'The congestion will be horrendous. It will take us hours and there's no guarantee of getting a tree. We've already lost two hours.'

'Okay then, let's head back home and face the music,' Flaky replies.

'Not on your nelly. I'm not giving up yet.'

'That's the spirit, Billy Boy. Don't listen to the quisling.'

'You have an uncanny knack of always leading us into trouble. You have a history of it,' Flaky gripes.

'Ignore him, Bill. That's typical of Flaky. He typecasts and pigeonholes people. He assumes their past behaviour has a bearing on their future endeavours.'

'He's right,' Robbo chirps, 'the future is not yet written.'

'I have a plan,' I say.

'Here we go. And does this plan involve sitting in a country pub drinking beer, by any chance?' Flaky asks in a holier-than-thou manner.

I glare at him. 'Not everything involves sitting in a pub drinking beer,' I snap.

'At last! I'm glad to hear it.'

4: God Rest Ye Merry Gentlemen

We're sitting in the Fox and Hounds sipping on pints of Timothy Taylor's finest bitter. It's located in a tiny village about five miles from the plantation.

'What's your masterplan?' Flaky asks as he takes a gulp of the amber nectar.

'I'm cogitating, give me time,' I reply. Geordie necks the last of his pint and slams his glass onto the table.

'Your shout, Flaky,' he states, licking his lips.

'But I've still got a half pint left?' he says, looking worried.

'Tough titties. If you wanna drink with the big boys then you keep up,' he replies as me and Robbo finish off our drinks and push our glasses towards Flaky.

'He's right, Flaky,' Robbo says. 'If you're in a round, you drink to the fastest drinker not the slowest.'

'I'll get you three another, but I'm okay,' he replies.

'Ah, ah… no. That's not the way it works,' Geordie responds. 'That way you're only buying three pints instead of four which means you're a tight arsed wuss.'

Flaky bristles. 'A wuss, am I?'

'That's what I said.' Flaky stands and pours the beer down his neck, quite literally, as a good portion of it trickles from the side of his mouth, down his chin and onto his jumper. He finishes, burps then wipes the drips from his chin on the back of his hand. He appears quite proud of himself, as if he's conquered Everest.

'Wuss indeed! Anyone can drink beer. You three think you're so big and tough, don't you? I can drink you all under the table.' He marches off towards the bar.

'Is that his second?' queries Robbo.

'Aye.'

'I think it might have gone to his head.'

'You're right, it has. He's forgotten he bought the last round before this. The man's clueless,' Geordie says, smirking.

'I need a smoke,' I announce.

'Me too,' says Robbo. 'Let's go outside.' We head towards the exit.

'Hey, Flaky!' I shout. 'We're going outside for a smoke. Bring the beers out!' Flaky turns and gives us the thumbs up.

We clear snow from a couple of benches and sit down at rustic wooden tables. We spark up—me a cigarette, Robbo… well, you know.

'What's the plan, then?' Geordie enquires.

'I'm still cogitating,' I reply.

'Don't cogitate too long. Time is ticking down.'

'Have I ever let you down yet?'

'Aye, on numerous occasions.' I ignore his barb as Flaky arrives with the drinks.

'As you know, I rarely have a tipple, but I must say this beer is quite moreish. It gives one a pleasant, exuberant, euphoric feeling.' I take a draft of beer as I gaze down the village street. A white, flatbed truck is heading our way.

'Take a look at that,' I say, nodding towards the truck.

38

'I'll be,' Geordie exclaims. On the back of the truck is an enormous Christmas tree, even taller than the one we nearly purloined.

'Must be destined for a village square somewhere,' Robbo adds.

'Nah,' I say. 'All the towns and villages erected their trees mid-November. It'll be going to someone's bloody mansion house.'

'Maybe we should follow it, flag the driver down and ask him where he got it from?'

'No point. It will have been ordered six months ago, and it's a commercial tree, you can tell by its size,' I say. We quickly finish our second pint, well, three of us at least. Flaky eventually forces his down and lets out another burp.

'Have you finished cogitating yet?' he asks, slurring his words, slightly.

I nod. 'There's another plantation about five miles west of Whitstone Village. They're mature trees, but there must be a rogue sapling or two knocking about somewhere. It doesn't matter how tall it is, even a four-footer will do. The kids won't notice at their age. Better something than nothing.'

'Is that it? Is that your grand masterplan?' Flaky whines.

'Can you stop with the negatude?' Geordie growls.

'Yeah, man,' begins Robbo, 'your negativity is like a nefarious raven with ominous intent swooping down on us all the time. It's like being at a Dickensian funeral.' We stare at him. That's what pot can do, kids—keep off it!

*****

The snow begins to fall again; silent, thick, heavy. As majestic as it is, it will not aide us in our quest for a tree. Thankfully, a snowplough has been through clearing the roads, but the conditions are still hazardous. Will Geordie heed the conditions? The answer is obvious.

'Geordie, slow down! We're on narrow country roads with blind bends, concealed entrances, and sub-zero temperatures,' I advise. He pays no attention to my instruction as we round a corner. Ahead, a truck pulls out of an entrance in front of us. Geordie hits the horn and brakes at the same time. The car veers and shimmies from side to side. We come to a sliding halt less than a foot away from the underside of the body of the truck. The truck driver and Geordie simultaneously wind their windows down and stick their heads out.

'You bloody moron!' shouts the truck driver. 'Drive to the conditions!'

'Hey, pal! It was my right of way!'

'Yeah, so what? It was a blind bend, you dickweed!'

'Dickweed, is it? I'll give you dickweed! Care to step out of that cab?' The trucky quickly pulls away. My heart resumes beating. 'The problem is people don't know the road rules. It was my right of way.'

'Yeah, I'll put that on your headstone; "Here lies Geordie Kincaid, decapitated by a flatbed truck on a wintry Christmas Eve. But he did have the right of way!" Hey, hang on a mo, was that the truck which passed through the village about ten minutes ago with the Christmas tree on the back?'

'I believe it was,' Flaky replies as he wipes a bead of sweat from his brow.

'Geordie, pull into the entrance.' He navigates the car into a large oval opening. A high brick wall demarcates the boundary of the property. Two giant, wrought-iron gates, supported by ancient brick piers, are open. There's a plaque affixed to the wall. It reads: "Cumberfutch Manor".

'Well, well, well,' sniffs Robbo. 'I think we've stumbled onto Lord Crumbletwats patch.'

'Payback time. Proceed, Jeeves,' I instruct. Flaky leans over from the back seat.

'I don't think this is a very good idea. If his Lordship is home, he could get our numberplate.'

'Hmm... good point. Although, I doubt he's back from his ride yet, but better safe than sorry. Geordie, do you have a screwdriver handy?'

'Aye, there's one in the glovebox.'

I grab the screwdriver and jump out of the car. Thirty seconds later, I toss the number plates into the boot. 'Drive on,' I order. As we near the manor house, we spot the giant Christmas tree laid out on the snow about ten feet away from the entrance. 'Okay, pull up here.'

'What's the plan, Bill? Shall we throw the tree onto the top of the car, quickly strap it down and take off?'

I think for a second. 'No. We need to be more adroit. Geordie, when you went to the toyshop in Skipton, did you get that police badge for Wallace?'

'Aye, and even better, I got a warrant card. The lad will be chuffed to bits tomorrow.'

'Give them to me.'

'What?'

'You heard. Hand them over.' He reaches into his trench coat and hands me the badge and warrant card. I pull my wallet out and drop them into the centre crease.

'I'm not sure what your game is, Will, but I want no part of it,' says Flaky.

'Suit yourself,' I respond. 'We're probably better off without you. Okay, boys, let's do this.'

'Oh, the three musketeers, is it? Don't think you're pushing me out of the game that easily!' Flaky exclaims, indignantly. We saunter to the imposing front door and I press the bell.

41

'What's the go?' asks Robbo.

'Not sure yet. Just play along. We'll wing it. Sometimes good results can be obtained by not knowing what the hell is going on.'

'You're doing a good job of it,' Geordie says, as he dons his Ushanka and fastens his trench coat against the cold.

'Thanks.' I study him as an idea begins to sprout. I ring the bell again. The door creaks open and we're confronted with an elderly, stooped gentleman, dressed in an old-fashioned butler's uniform.

'Hello, gentlemen. How may I help you?' I pull out my wallet and flash the child's police badge at him, followed by the warrant card.

'I'm DCI Lennon from the fraud squad,' I announce in a commanding voice. I point at Geordie. 'This is special agent, Andropov Kalashnikov, Russian attaché to Interpol'. I turn to Robbo and Flaky. 'And these are Sergeant McCartney and Constable Harrison from the dog squad.'

'Oh dear,' he replies, perturbed by the run of events. 'How can I help you?'

'Is Lord Fumblecrutch at home?'

'No, I'm sorry, he isn't. He went out for a canter and is not due back for at least another half hour.'

'What about Lady Crumblestick? Is she at home?'

'I'm afraid not. Lady Cumberfutch left us last year.'

'Hmm, I see. How very convenient.'

'Can I ask what all this is about?' he says, in a brittle tremulous voice.

'Who are you and what's your name?' I demand.

'I'm Jitters, the butler to Lord Cumberfutch.'

42

'Is that so, old man? I'm afraid to inform you you're at the epicentre of an international fraud investigation. Is that Christmas tree yours?' I say, pointing at the giant pine laid in the snow.

'Yes. It was delivered not more than five minutes ago.'

'Hmm… just as I thought. Are you aware it's stolen property?'

'No, of course not.'

'You're a good liar.'

'I'm sorry, but I don't understand?' He's not the only one. I pause for a breath and some thinking time.

'We have reason to believe that Lord Cummerbund is the head of an international crime syndicate that smuggles Christmas trees across continents. And you, my friend, are up to your armpits in trouble. That tree was reported stolen from Red Square four days ago and has caused an international diplomatic spat of epic proportions. The Russian Army, as we speak, is massing on the borders of Ukraine and Belarus. We are but one accidental gunshot away from the beginning of World War 3. Do you want that on your conscience? Come, come, man… what have you got to say for yourself?'

'I'm not sure what to say. We normally order our tree from Arkwright's in Harrogate.'

'I see, playing coy, eh? Do you think you can take us for fools?'

'No, I mean yes, oh Lord, I'm not sure what I mean.'

'So, you want to play hardball, eh? Special agent Kalashnikov, what are your thoughts?' I say, turning to Geordie.

'Ya vol, Kapitain, nadia comaneci unt chechen perestroika vladivostock. Garee unt kasparov net olga korbet?'

'Net,' I reply.

'Ich bin ein Berliner glauben apfel gritzen unt flauzenshizen?'

'What did he say?' the butler asks.

'He suspects you may be the German ringleader, the mafia boss, the Don, the head coach, the Man from Delmonte.'

'Oh dear, I think there's been some misunderstanding.'

'I'll be the judge of that.'

'Maybe I should call PC McGarrity. He's our local constable based in Skipton. I'm sure he'd be able to clear all this up.'

'Don't bother! McGarrity is a plant. He's been covertly watching this place for the last fourteen months and he's just been transferred to Stalingrad.'

'My word! And he only had a few weeks to go before retirement.'

'Sleazen unt kable de Liechtenstein. Unt fontzwarp grunt rot oktober?' Geordie says, in almost perfect Russian.

'What did he say?' the butler asks.

'He said we should take you in for questioning.'

'But I have a meat and potato pie warming in the oven.'

I return my gaze to Geordie. 'Net. Sozplowshenietche et lada, et odin monkien, di organ, gritzchen, gritzchen, gritzchen!'

'And what did you say?'

'I told him we're after the organ grinder, not the monkey.' There's the click of a lighter followed by the smell of weed. The butler peers over my shoulder at Robbo and Flaky. Geordie bends down and sticks his face in front of the visibly shaken butler.

'Et zietgrab untz flatustuber! Blitzen, smitzen, panza, danzer unt Rudolph. Net, el sprockenzedeutsche!'

I nod at Geordie. 'Hmm... possibly. Unfurbergluber et yeltsin sputnik... net.'

'What now?' Jitters asks, getting shakier by the second.

'He said that you remind him of his Uncle Rudolph, an elderly gentleman with a goitre. Apparently, a keen golfer with a handicap of ten. Played a few games as centre forward for Dynamo Kiev, but underneath, a criminal mastermind. I'm afraid we're going to have to confiscate the Christmas tree.'

'I'm not sure Lord Cumberfutch will be happy about that.'

'The world is hours away from Armageddon and you're worried Lord Flubbercrutch may not be happy! Do you want to be remembered as the man who caused the destruction of the world?'

'No, not really. I'm not sure that would go down too well at my croquet club. It's our centenary next summer.'

'It won't be much fun playing croquet on a radioactive dust bowl, will it?'

'No, it wouldn't. It was only reseeded last spring.'

'Indeed! That tree needs to be impounded, immediately. We'll escort it down to the station for questioning, fingerprinting and DNA analysis. You can also inform Lord Cumquickley, upon his return, that he is under house arrest and must surrender his passport. We'll be back tomorrow to interrogate him, and it won't be pleasant. It will involve nipple clamps, a ball-gag, and rather large gooseberries. Now, you behave, otherwise you'll find yourself working twenty-five hour shifts in the salt mines of Siberia for the next ten-years.'

'My word! Would I be able to take Mr Tiddles with me? He's a very good mouser.'

'Sorry. No pets allowed. Cat flu is rampant over there. Right then, I hope I've made myself clear?'

'Yes, perfectly.'

'Good. Well, enjoy the rest of your day and I bid you farewell.'

'Gdansk,' nods Geordie. The butler totters back into the house and closes the door.

'Quick lads, let's get this bloody Christmas tree onto the car and scarper—pronto!'

It takes a good fifteen-minutes to manoeuvre the massive tree onto the roof rack and strap it down. The tip of the tree is bent almost double and attached to the tow bar. The trunk juts out a good three feet past the bonnet.

'Good work, men! See what we can achieve when we work as a team? Let's get the hell out of here. It's nearly four o'clock. We were only supposed to be nipping out for an hour.' We jump into the car and fasten our seatbelts.

'Geordie, remember the conditions. Let's get home in one piece. Softly, softly, catchee monkey,' I say.

'What does that mean?'

'I'm not sure. Just go!' He sets off carefully down the driveway as the snowfall intensifies. The unwanted sight of Lord Cumberfutch materialises as we near the gates. He rocks gently from side to side in his saddle. A rope, attached to his horse, pulls our original Christmas tree along behind it. He smiles and nods at us, unaware of who we are.

'Shit the bed! Avert your gaze,' Geordie murmurs. 'He doesn't know it's us.' As we pass by the Lord of the Manor, his smile is wiped from his face and replaced with a look of thunder.

'Geordie, I think he's rumbled us. Put your foot down!'

'Make your bloody mind up. One minute it's drive carefully, the next it's put your foot down.' As he hits the accelerator, the Range Rover swerves from side to side, making little purchase with the snowy driveway, despite being a four-wheel drive. I glance in the rear-view mirror. Lord Grumblesnatch dismounts from the horse, grabs his shotgun, and takes aim.

'Duck!' I cry.

'Where?' Robbo shouts.

'No, bob down, you moron!' Two rapid blasts from the shotgun are instantly followed by the sound of breaking glass and the pit-a-pat of pellets penetrating metal.

'Geordie, floor it!' I scream as I witness his Lordship deftly reload his gun. We pass through the gates.

'Turn left!' I shout.

'But it's right to Whitstone!' Geordie cries.

'It's a ruse!' I respond.

'A what?'

'A ploy, a feign, a tactic! He'll think we're going left and jump in his car to follow us. By the time he's run into the house to grab his car keys, we'll have turned around and be heading the opposite way.'

'Nice one, Billy Boy! Always the man with a plan.'

*****

After the initial adrenalin rush, we calm down, slightly. I'm berated on the journey back to Whitstone by Flaky.

'It was reprehensible the way you treated that geriatric butler. The poor man. He's obviously suffering from some affliction. He was shaking when he first opened the door. By the time you and Geordie had finished your pathetic impersonations, the man was a quivering mess. It wouldn't surprise me if he has a heart attack thanks to you.' As much as I hate to say it, I sort of agree with him.

'Yeah, well, sometimes you've gotta do what you've gotta do, for the greater good, i.e. a Christmas tree for our kids.' We enter the outskirts of Whitstone, and I spot the alluring lights of the Beaconsfield Arms in the distance. 'Actually, I've been having a crisis of conscience ever since we left

47

Cumberfutch Manor. I propose we stop off at the pub to reflect on our actions. All those in favour raise their right arm and say, aye.'

'Give me strength,' Flaky sighs. 'I give in. It's like herding cats— impossible.' Three arms are raised, followed by three ayes.

'The ayes have it. Carried unanimously,' Geordie confirms.

*****

'Let me briefly recap,' Flaky begins. 'We left the house, crashed the car, visited a pub. Shopped in Skipton, visited a pub. Cut down a tree, got caught trespassing, visited a pub. Traumatised an ageing butler, stole another tree and visited another pub—do you see a common thread to these events?' Flaky asks in his most patronising manner. Geordie and Robbo scratch their heads.

'I'm not sure what you're getting at,' Geordie responds.

'Nor me,' Robbo agrees. 'They're all random events. Life, the universe, it's all random. There's no point trying to find meaning out of any of it. Everything is chaos.'

'You're bloody right when you lot get together!'

'Stop your blether, man, and get the drinks in,' Geordie says as he finishes his pint and wipes the suds from his top lip onto the back of his coat.

'Hang on, I got the one before last.'

'So? We've gone full circle. Now it starts again in reverse order. Don't you know anything about drinking etiquette?' Flaky reluctantly collects the empty glasses and saunters over to the bar.

With our pints replenished, we begin our discussion.

'What's praying on your mind, Bill? Is it the butler? We did give him a bit of a fright.'

'Yes, but it's not just that, there's something else. I didn't take much notice at the time, but I've been thinking.'

'About?' Robbo says as he takes a hefty quaff of his beer.

'When I asked Jitters if Lady Cumberfutch was at home, he said that she'd left last year. I assumed he meant she'd walked out, you know, left the miserable old bugger. But what if he didn't mean that?'

'You think he meant she'd died, passed away?' Flaky says.

'Yes. And Geordie, when we were on Fallside Gap and you asked the Lord what had made him so bitter and twisted, do you remember his response?'

'Aye, it was a bit odd. His eyes seemed to glaze over, he appeared almost wistful.'

'Oh, dear. What have we done?' Flaky says mournfully. 'If it's true, if his wife has recently departed, he must be in a world of pain and anguish.'

'Imagine if one of our wives had died, how would we feel?' Robbo says.

'What should we do?' Geordie asks.

'I think we should return the tree and apologise. I have a plastic tree in the attic, we'll have to make do with that this year. It's not such a big deal.'

'Oh, come on Bill, you know what his type are like, he's not going to forgive and forget. He'll have the law onto us.'

'His type?'

'Yeah, you know, privileged, entitled, to the manor born—quite literally in his case.'

'He's still human, with feelings. Anyway, it's not about what happens to us, it's about doing the right thing. All those in favour of returning the tree raise their right arms and say, aye.' Four arms are reluctantly raised followed by four ayes. 'Okay, let's sup up and go and dance with the devil.'

5: In The Deep Mid-Winter

We park up outside Cumberfutch Manor and alight from the car as his Lordship appears on the doorstep brandishing his bloody shotgun. Jitters is behind him. We amble over.

'The brigands return. What is it this time? Come to knock off the family silver or a few oil paintings?' he says with that deep emotionless voice and stoic intensity.

'No,' I begin, 'we've come to return your tree and apologise. We were in the wrong. Things got a little out of hand.'

'Really? Trespass, theft, vandalism, impersonating police officers, scaring an eighty-year-old man half to death and you think you can waltz up here and ask for forgiveness?'

'They do say that forgiveness is a healing power,' Flaky states.

'Do they, indeed? Here, hold this Jitters and keep it trained on them. If they make any sudden moves—shoot,' he says as he hands the shotgun to his butler. Jitters is shaking like a shitting dog, and I fear the gun could go off at any moment. Lord Cumberfutch pulls out his mobile phone. 'You're lucky. The weather has favoured you. I've tried ringing our local constable a few times, but I can't seem to get through. I surmise he's busy with trapped motorists and car accidents. I'll give him another go. I'm not sure he'll get here today, so you may have one more night of freedom.' He squints at his phone.

'I wouldn't do that if I were you,' I say.

'Oh, and why's that?'

51

'Our acts were petty misdemeanours, unlike yours. Firing two rounds at a car with four people inside is a far more serious offence. You could have seriously injured one of us... or worse. I dare say that through your contacts you may escape a prison sentence but imagine the gossip around the Dales, and the House of Lords, for that matter. Not a good look.' His eyes bore into me.

'Touché. It seems we have reached an impasse. I may have underestimated you. I thought you were a bunch of louts, but obviously not.' He slips his mobile away, takes the gun from Jitters, uncocks it and leans it against the wall of the house. 'As it's the time of year for peace, love and forgiveness, I'll accept your apology, on one condition.'

'What?' I say.

'My stable hand hasn't been able to get through because of the snow, he usually helps me with the tree. Therefore, I'd like your assistance. I need to get the tree inside the house and erected.'

I smile at him. 'Not a problem.' He glances over his shoulder at the tree from Fallside Gap that is laying on the driveway.

'There's no point letting that one go to waste. You may as well take it. We'll untie the one on your car and swap them over.'

*****

I'm sweating like a stuck pig. We push, pull and cajole the damn tree into its stand in the cavernous entrance hall as Lord Cumberfutch barks orders at us.

'No, not there, to the right man, to the right!' We drag the blasted tree to the right. 'Watch the bloody painting! That's an original Picasso, it's priceless. No, to the left a little more, to the left, I say!' As we pull it back to the left, Geordie stumbles and bangs into a stand holding a large vase. Lord Cumberfutch rushes forward. 'Damn it, man!' He catches it mid fall. 'That's an imperial Ming vase! It's over five-hundred-years old!'

'Lucky it's not new then,' the simpleton replies.

'Watch the chandelier, the chandelier, the damned chandelier! Bring it forward a touch. No! Not that much. I said a touch, man, a touch! Okay, stop right there, yes, perfect, splendid!' We stand back and admire the tree. It's a beauty!

'How do you decorate it?' Robbo asks.

'I have an extraordinary long pair of stepladders but there'll be no decorations this year. It can stand proud in all its natural glory.' I glance at the boys and nod my head covertly towards the doorway. His Lordship seems to have drifted into a reverie as he stands in front of the tree staring at it.

'I guess we better get going. Still a lot of work ahead of us,' I say. He drifts back from his trance.

'Yes, of course. I'll show you to the door.' As we walk down the hallway I notice a large framed photo on the wall. It's of Lord Cumberfutch in his younger days with a beautiful woman by his side. I assume it's his wife.

'Is that your wife?' I ask. He stops and gazes reflectively at the photograph.

'Yes,' he whispers.

'She's beautiful.'

'Yes, she was beautiful. I'm afraid breast cancer took her just over a year ago. Forty years together as man and wife.'

'That's a lifetime,' I say.

'Yes, it is. Funny how time flies. It only seems like yesterday I was taking her out on our first date. We had a picnic at Bolton Abbey. It was springtime, sunny and rich with the scent of daffodils in bloom. The River Wharfe was in full flow. We were completely alone. She'd made cucumber sandwiches and a flask of tea. Funny how you remember the little things. I was the luckiest man in the world.'

53

The other boys stroll past in silence. Geordie stops at another photograph hanging on the wall.

'Is this your lad?' he asks. The Lord walks over to him.

'Yes, that's Michael.'

'What regiment is he in?'

'He was in the Royal Engineers, a Captain. Deployed to Afghanistan in 2013. A roadside bomb got him. He'd just turned thirty. A futile waste of life lost in a futile war.'

'As in so many wars,' Geordie murmurs.

'Indeed.' Geordie reaches out and places his big mitt on the Lord's shoulder and gently squeezes it.

'I'm sorry for your loss. There can be nothing worse than losing a child. It doesnae matter what age they are, they're still your bairns.' Lord Cumberfutch gazes at the big fella.

'Never a truer word spoken.' There's a heavy silence for a moment.

I cough. 'Ahem, we better get going,' I say. We troop down the hallway as though tiptoeing on eggshells. Lord Cumberfutch opens the door for us. 'Sorry about before, you know, the tree and what not.'

'It's all water under the bridge now. Maybe if I'd taken the time to listen to your reasons, we could have avoided all this argy-bargy. And I apologise for shooting at you. It was foolhardy and reckless. I haven't been in the best of places, lately, mentally. Still, it's no excuse.' He turns to Geordie. 'You can send me the bill for any damage, and I'll take care of it.'

'Nah, don't you worry about a thing. That's what insurance is for.' They exchange warm smiles.

'I say, I don't suppose you boys would care for a quick snifter before you leave? I have an excellent bottle of Old Admiral Brandy that I've been meaning to crack open, but never had a good reason to do so.' I'm really itching to go, so I give Geordie the "it's time to go," nod. He sends a sly wink back.

'That's very kind of you, your Lordship, why not, only the one though, then we really must be on our way,' Geordie replies. Obviously, something was lost in translation.

'Excellent! Follow me this way. I have a roaring log fire going in my study. It's where I spend most of my time these days. Far cosier than the rest of the house. I'll get Jitters to bring us some mince pies to go with the brandy. Oh, and please, call me Stanley.'

*****

So much for a quick snifter. We polish off the bottle of brandy in no time and Stanley cracks open another one, this time peach brandy which is quite addictive. We regale the Lord with tales of our misadventures over the past few years which has him in howls of laughter. There's the story of how we trashed three classic antique cars belonging to a famous Hollywood producer. How Geordie nearly drowned in the Mediterranean and the account of Flaky's kidnapping by London gangsters and our cack-handed attempt to free him. I can assure you, none of those events were the slightest bit amusing when they happened. But with the passage of time and copious amounts of alcohol coursing through our veins, we can now see the funny side. I glance at my watch—6 pm—holy crap!

'Right, boys. We really need to go.'

'What's your rush?' chuckles Geordie, who is in an excessively boisterous mood.

'It's six o'clock. We left at midday to get a Christmas tree. We've been gone six hours.'

'So?' he replies, unperturbed.

'Our wives?' I say. His gormless grin disappears as a wave of panic shoots across his face. He jumps to his feet.

55

'Aye, we better go.' Robbo has nearly nodded off and Flaky is completely smashed and giggling like a child. I pull Robbo to his feet.

'Hey, what's wrong, man?' he mumbles.

'Time to go home and get the Christmas tree up,' I say. Stanley escorts us to the door.

'Wait!' I cry as a realisation dawns on me.'

'What is it?' Flaky giggles.

'We can't drive, we're all well over the limit.'

'Don't talk daft, Bill. I'm as fresh as a Daisy,' Geordie says.

'No, you're not. You're half-cut. What will Jackie say when she finds out you've been driving while pissed?' Again, the flash of panic.

'Aye, you're probably right. We'll ring for a taxi.'

'What about the tree?' Robbo murmurs. Damn it all! I fumble in my jacket for my phone.

'Geordie, you ring Jackie and tell her to come and get us.'

'Like hell I will! Do you think I've got a death wish?'

'Robbo, ring Julie and tell her where we are?'

'Oh, no, definitely not! She's got a hell of a temper on her. Why don't you ring Fiona?' he says.

'Aye, give Fiona a call, she'll collect us.'

'No, she'll be, ahem, she'll be busy. Anyway, I can't find my phone, I must have left it at home.'

'You can use mine,' says Geordie helpfully. He searches his pockets to no avail. 'Damn it! I think it's on charge in the bedroom. Robbo, lend Billy your phone.'

'No can do. I also left my phone behind. I'd have thought one of you idiots would have brought one with you.' Flaky is now busy at the end of the hallway talking to the Christmas tree.

'Not to worry,' says Stanley you can use mine. He hands me his mobile. It appears muggins, here, is the one to receive the initial ear bashing. I stare at the phone blankly.

'What's wrong?' Robbo asks.

'I don't know her number,' I mumble.

Geordie snorts his derision. 'You don't know your wife's phone number? What sort of excuse is that?'

'Honestly, I don't. I press her image when I call her. Do either of you two know your wife's numbers off by heart?' They both exchange glances. 'Hmm... I thought not.' I hand Stanley his mobile phone. 'Flaky! Have you got your phone on you?' He comes staggering towards us and pulls his phone from his jacket.

'I never go anywhere without it?' he slurs.

'Give Gillian a call and ask her to pick us up.'

'I think you'll be too heavy for her,' he titters.

'Stop being a prick and phone her now,' Geordie orders. He doesn't appear as boisterous as he did a few minutes ago.

'Ooh, touchy, touchy, big man. No need to get aggressive. Politeness will get you everywhere,' Flaky says, swaying from side to side. I snatch the phone from him and click on the image of his wife. I notice he's got about ten missed calls and texts, and his phone is set to silent. It rings as I hand it back to him.

'Hello, Gillian, it's me, your husband. You do remember me, don't you?' he snickers. 'What? Yes, of course we're all right. No, no, nothing's happened. The tree? Hang on, I'll check.' He swallows hard and staggers forward. 'She wants to know if we've got the tree?'

'Yes! Of course, we bloody have, you idiot!' Geordie yells.

'Yes! Of course, we bloody have, you idiot! No, not you dear, I was repeating what Geordie said. Drinking? I may have had a wee dram or two. No, I know I don't normally drink. Where am I? That's a damn good question. I'll ask.' He gazes at me. His head has taken on a life of its own as it flops forward one second, then snaps upright the next. 'Where am I, I mean us, I mean we?'

'You're at Lord Cumberfutch's Manor house about 15 miles from Whitstone,' I say, my patience wearing extremely thin.

Flaky burps and gives me the thumbs up. 'We're at Lord Chunderflutch, Hunderbutch, Cundersuch Manor. He's a terribly decent chap. He tried to shoot us. No, we're fine. Oh, I managed to get some vegan cheese...' I snatch the phone from him.

'Hi, Gillian, it's Will. Listen, we can't drive, we're all a tad over the limit so best not to risk it. I'll text you through the address and can one of you come and collect us?'

'Okay, Will. I'll set off straight away you text the address through.'

'Thanks Gillian, you're a star.'

'Hey, Bill?' Geordie says.

'What?'

'Tell her to take your car. It's got the sat nav. It'll be safer than looking at her phone.'

'Good idea. Gillian, bring my car, it's got built in sat nav. Then we'll exchange vehicles once you're here. The tree is on top of the Range Rover.'

'Okay, Will. I'm glad you're okay.'

'Yeah, we're all good. Hey, listen, how are the other girls? You know their mood?' There's silence. 'Gillian?'

'Send me the address and I'll see you soon.' I hand the phone back to Flaky who is grinning like one of those clowns at the fair, that you try and throw ping-pong balls into.

'What did she say when you asked about the girls?' Geordie asks, with a pained expression.

'Silence.'

'Oh, sweet merry Jesus!'

'Would you care for one more while you await your carriage?' Stanley asks.

'Thanks, but no thanks. A jug of water, four glasses and some strong coffee wouldn't go amiss, though.'

6: Ding Dong Merrily On High

It's a bitterly cold and frosty night, but nowhere near as cold and frosty as the reception that greets us as we troop into the kitchen. Luckily, there are plenty of children around to prevent an all out verbal assault.

'Where the hell have you been?' Fiona spits. 'We've been worried sick about you. We weren't far off from ringing the police. Why didn't you answer your phones?'

'Only Flaky had a phone, and it was on silent.'

'You could have rung us on that?'

'We didn't think.'

'No, that's right, you didn't bloody think!'

'Where's the tree?' Jackie barks.

'On top of the car,' I reply. The girls stare out of the window.

'You have got to be joking! How in hell's name do you expect to fit it into the living room?'

'Geordie had a better idea. We thought we'd put it outside next to the porch. It will look nice with lights on and real snow. It will last longer, and we won't have any pine needles to clean up.'

'You should know better than to listen to my husband's half-baked, pea-brained, infantile suggestions!' Jackie snipes, as Geordie visibly shrinks behind me.

'You were given one job to do, just the one!' joins in Julie. 'Get a tree! You've been gone over six hours. You could have grown a bloody tree in that time.'

'Let me explain,' Geordie begins.

'Shut up, you big dolt!' Jackie snaps. 'I don't want any explanations.' Flaky staggers forward. 'I thought you were going to keep them on the straight and narrow?' Jackie says, prodding Flaky in the chest.

'Ah, you see, the thing about cats is…' He stops abruptly, confused disorientated and swaying like a sapling in a hurricane. 'I can't remember what I was going to say,' he hiccups, slurring his words like a drunken sailor.

'He's legless,' Gillian says. 'In all the years we've been together, I've never seen him as drunk as this.'

'My God!' Jackie exclaims. 'How much have you lot had to drink? You must have been sat in the pub all day!'

'Don't use Flaky as a barometer,' Geordie says. 'He gets pissed on the whiff of a wine gum. We've had a couple of beers and one or two drams of brandy—that's all.'

'I think everyone needs to take a chill pill,' Robbo starts. 'It's not the time for bad vibes, and negative emotions. It's Christmas Eve, after all. Good tidings to all men, bearing gifts and bringing light into the world.' He receives a quick slap around the head from Julie.

'Don't tell us to take a chill pill, you inconsiderate drunken space cadet. We've been stuck in this kitchen all day cooking and chasing around after the kids while you lot went swanning off to the pub. Get out of my sight!'

'Whoa! That's some negative karma you're throwing my way, girl!' I step between Robbo and his wife as I fear the next thing she could be throwing is her fist down the stoner's throat.

'I don't suppose there's any food on the go?' Geordie asks expectantly, completely misreading the situation.

'What do you think!' Jackie yells.

'Slim to no chance?'

'Correct!' We try to slink off through the kitchen, but Jackie isn't finished yet. She blocks Geordie and leans towards him, her face mere millimetres away from his reddish nose.

'Listen up and listen good, big man... this is what's going to happen; you and your three sidekicks are going to put the Christmas tree up, with lights on. Then you're going to bathe the children and get them into their pyjamas. After that, you will go from room to room and clean and tidy everything up and vacuum and mop the floors. At 9:30 you'll dress up as Santa as planned. Once the children are all safely in bed, fast asleep, then you may get some food.

Is there any part of that you don't understand? I want to make sure my instructions are crystal clear so even four drunken dickheads can comprehend them.' We all glance at each other. 'WELL!'

'Yep, we understand, don't we boys?' Geordie mumbles, gazing at the floor. Three of us eagerly nod our heads, as Flaky steadies himself on the kitchen benchtop.

'Oh, and one last thing. If we catch any of you having another drink, even a sip, then we will gladly castrate you. No more alcohol until dinnertime tomorrow? Is that also crystal clear?' We all gulp and nod at the same time.

'Yes, dear,' Geordie replies, sheepishly. 'We'll go out the back and start clearing the snow away so we can get the tree up.'

We leave the hostile territory of the kitchen and move into the safe zone of the back garden. We zip our coats, don our hats and pull our gloves on.

'It's a bloody chilly night,' Robbo grumbles.

'We'll soon warm up once we get started,' Geordie says. 'What's the plan of attack, Bill?'

'There's two shovels in the shed, a heavy-duty cast iron stand for the tree, Christmas lights, extension lead, oh, and we'll also need a drill and some bolts to secure the stand to the pavers. We don't want the bloody thing toppling over on us.' Flaky has already slumped onto a bench seat, staring happily out into the dark night.

'It's beautiful,' he murmurs to himself.

'You do realise he'll be about as much use as a chocolate fireguard?' Geordie says.

'Yep. We'll have to do it without him. I reckon if we put our backs into it, and work as a team, we can finish it in an hour.'

'Okay, sounds good, Bill. But first, may I suggest we retire to the studio and gird our loins with a quick bottle or two of refreshing lager to blow the cobwebs away,' he says rubbing his hands together.

'You heard what Jackie said.'

'Ha! You don't think I'm scared of that lot in there, do you?' he scoffs, jutting his thumb over his shoulder towards the house.

'It looked like it, from where I was standing,' Robbo says.

'That was just an act, sunshine! Let them feel a sense of superiority—it never fails. The truth is, they can't speak to us like that. We're international rock stars! We've sold millions of records all over the world. We've headlined at Glastonbury, filled to capacity - Madison Square Gardens! The world's media awaits with bated breath on our incoherent mumblings about world events and the meaning of life! We are living heroes. Now is not the time for faint-heartedness, capitulation, nor surrender!'

'Thank you, Mr Churchill. The fact is when we're at home we have no power. We're just the random guy who empties the bins and checks the oil level in the car,' I reply.

'He's right, Geordie. You can win a battle overseas but in your own living room—it's game-over.'

Geordie glares at us. 'Hmm… I see. Spineless cuckolds. I'd have expected that sort of attitude from Flaky but not you guys. Is this what it's come to? Well, you two may like to strut around in a skirt in your own home, but I wear the trousers in my marriage—and she knows it!'

'GEORDIE!' Jackie's voice is like the boom of cannon fire.

'Yes, dear?' he replies as he nervously scratches at the stubble on his chin.

'We're getting short on wood for the fire. Bring some more logs in before you start on the Christmas tree!'

'Of course, my love. I'll be there in a jiffy.' He waits a few seconds until he's confident she's retreated back inside. 'Okay… the coast is clear. Time for those refreshing ales, then we'll work like three tigers.'

*****

Robbo is busy clearing snow away as Geordie and I position the tree stand, and mark pilot holes into the pavers. We quickly drill four holes, secure the bolts through the stand and into the bricks, then give it a kick to test its sturdiness.

'Jobs a good 'un,' says Geordie. As I stand, I slip on the ground that Robbo has cleared.

'Damn it; ice,' I say.

'Have you any grit?'

'Yeah, back of the shed.'

'Take a look at those two wankers,' Geordie says, nodding first towards Flaky who's laid out on the bench fast asleep and Robbo who is bent double and making little progress with clearing the snow. 'Bloody useless, the pair of them.' He grabs the second shovel, walks up behind Robbo and thwacks him hard on the arse with it.

'Out of my way, Noddy. Tits on a bull. You go to the shed and grab the bag of grit and spread it over the cleared areas.'

'Hey! That's uncool, man!' he yells, rubbing his backside.

'Shut your cake-hole and get the grit.' As Robbo walks past me, he lights a spliff. I snatch it from his mouth and toss into the snow.

'What the?'

'You're not much use to us now, but you'll be worse if you're spaced out. You can have one when we've finished.' He trundles off, moaning about infringement of liberties.

We've reached a critical juncture in proceedings. The Christmas tree is lying next to its stand already festooned in Christmas lights. Now is the moment of truth. A rope is attached to the top of the tree which Robbo is going to pull on once me and Geordie have lifted it up a little. Geordie will then take control of the trunk and I, the mid-section. Once in place, we have metal pegs to drive through the stand and into the trunk.

'Okay boys, ready?' Robbo and Geordie nod. 'After three; one, two, three.' The thing weighs a ton, and it takes every ounce of our strength to raise it up to a forty-five-degree angle. 'Right, Robbo, pull!' The tree begins to rise to its full height.

'Billy, Robbo, hold it right there while I drive the pegs in.' There's the clank of steel against steel as Geordie works feverishly at securing the tree. 'Okay, let go of the rope and see how she is?' Robbo releases the rope as I stand back.

'Looking good, Geordie,' I say. 'Perfectly straight.'

'Give it a good old push. See if it moves.' I give the tree a shove, but it's rock solid.

'Mission accomplished,' I say. We stand back and admire our handiwork. The tip of the tree is about level with the guttering.

'Jeez, she's a big bugger!' Geordie says chuckling. 'Right, switch the lights on.'

'Robbo, you wanna do the honours?' Robbo flips the switch, and the tree comes alive in soft whites, blues, oranges and reds, as powdery flakes of snow settle on its welcoming branches. A gentle snoring distracts us. We gaze over at Flaky. Geordie sports a mischievous grin as he picks up a handful of snow and moulds it into a tight ball, then repeats the process. Very daintily, he places one ball over each of Flaky's eyes.

'You rotten bastard,' I whisper.

'Serves him right,' Geordie giggles.

'Geordie,' Jackie shouts making him jump. He turns towards the back door.

'Yes, dear?'

'Have you seen the second phone charger?'

'Yes, it's in the glove box.'

'Throw me the keys.' Geordie fumbles in his pocket and tosses the keys into the air. Jackie catches them one handed and disappears back inside.

'I think we deserve a beer or two for our sterling efforts, don't you?' Geordie says.

'You're pushing it, pal, but okay.' He quickly returns with three beers, cracks the tops off and hands them out. We are mid glug when Jackie's voice booms out again.

'GEORDIE!' Her pitch and volume indicate trouble ahead. There's an expulsion of beer into the night sky.

'Shit, hide the beer,' Geordie says, as he spins around in circles, completely bewildered. We both press our beers onto Robbo.

'Where can I hide them?' he says, in a state of alarm.

'Unless you want to kiss goodbye to your gonads, I suggest you find somewhere in the next few seconds,' Geordie says, panicking. I look around for a good hiding spot.

'Stick them in Flaky's jacket pockets.'

'What the hell as happened to the car?' Jackie shouts, appearing behind us as though she's been teleported there.

'I'm quite sure I don't know what you mean, dear?' Geordie says, looking hurt.

'There's two massive dints in the passenger side doors. The taillight is broken. There're dimples in the boot. The roof rack is mangled, the numberplates are missing, the roof is scratched, and there's resin all over the bonnet. And the inside smells disgusting—it's like a cross between a brewery, a hashish parlour and a man's urinal!'

'Don't worry, pet. The insurance will pay for it.'

'And what about the £4000 excess?'

'The what?'

'The excess. We have to pay the first £4000 of any claim.'

'I've never heard of that before,' he says as he removes his Ushanka and scratches his noggin. She moves towards him as he takes a tentative step back.

'What buffoonery did you lot get up to today?' she demands, jabbing her finger at him.

'Let me ex… let me explain,' he stammers. She holds her palm in front of him.

'No! I don't want to hear it—not tonight. It can wait. We'll have a thorough investigation on Boxing Day.' She presses her finger and thumb together. 'You are this close from really copping it… just one more thing, I swear to God.' She turns and stomps off.

'You really put her in her place. How's your skirt? Not too draughty, I hope?' Robbo says.

'Sod off,' Geordie mumbles. There's a long sorrowful groan as Flaky stirs. As he sits up the two snowballs fall from his eyes. He leans back in the bench.

'Oh, oh, I'm dying. My head. What's happening? I can't open my eyes. I think they're frozen to the inside of my skull. Why are my pants wet? How did these beer bottles get here? Why is everything spinning? I need to go to bed.'

I grab him under one arm and Geordie the other and we manoeuvre him inside, up the stairs and to his bedroom, where Gillian is waiting to undress him and put him to bed.

'Thanks, boys,' she says with a caring smile. 'I'll take over from here. I can't be too cross with him. He's never done this before. Maybe he wanted to let his hair down for once.' We leave her to it and close the door behind us.

'How come numbnuts gets the caring, understanding wife?' Geordie asks.

'Luck of the draw, I guess.'

*****

The three of us work our butts off for the next hour. We get the kids into their baths, then tackle downstairs. Toys and detritus are collected and dropped into plastic boxes, then deposited in the children's wardrobes. Carpets are vacuumed, hard floors are swept and mopped. The kitchen is cleaned from top to bottom. We do a wonderful job, if I say so myself, and I do.

The kids are mesmerised by the giant Christmas tree and more importantly, so are the women. We have just about ingratiated our way back into their good books. At one point, we all even get a kiss from our respective spouses as we stand under the mistletoe that dangles from the hallway ceiling.

However, don't you find that life has a way of playing with your head? Just when you think you're in the clear, fate opens the man hatch to your armoured vehicle and lobs a hand grenade inside.

Fiona has returned from the front yard after depositing a bag of rubbish into the bin.

'Will,' she begins, hesitantly, as I'm wrapping the power cord around the vacuum.

'Yes, Fiona?'

'Where's our car?'

'It's at Lord Cumberfutch's Manor. Why? You're not worried about it, are you? It will be safe there. We can collect it tomorrow or the day after.' She crosses her arms, pouts, and begins to tap her foot aggressively on the floor. Never a good sign. The other women slowly drift to her side, like she's just beaten the jungle drums. Robbo and Geordie spot the signals and fall in behind me as though I'm a heat shield. 'Is it a problem?'

'A problem? No, why would it be a problem? It's gone 8:30 and in approximately eleven hours five little children will wake up and rush downstairs to see what Santa has put in their sacks.'

'Your point being?'

'My point is that Santa won't have left them anything. Their sacks will be empty.' I'm feeling quite heady. I try to laugh but it sounds more like the final expulsion of air from a dying man.

'How do you work that out?' I say. Gillian, Jackie and Julie all clasp their hands to their mouths, in perfect unison as a look of abject terror illuminates their faces. They are one step ahead of me and my dim-witted friends because we haven't got a bloody clue what's going on. Fiona's pout is increasing in size.

'Because, in the boot of our car are the children's presents.'

'Oh, I'm so sorry Fiona! That was my fault!' cries Gillian. 'I took your car because Will said it had built in sat nav.'

'It was actually Geordie's idea,' I correct. 'I was just passing it on.'

'Don't bring me into this. You're on your own here, pal,' whispers Geordie.

'Sorry Gillian, I don't blame you in the slightest. You drew the short straw by having to collect the nincompoops in the first place. It can't have been very pleasant. No, I blame my husband.' There's an audible sigh of relief from behind.

'And his three idiot friends,' adds Jackie, who has now struck a similar pose to Fiona. I'm lost for words, as are my two loyal companions who seem to have shrunk to the size of mice and lost the power of communication.

'The girls and I are going upstairs now for a pamper and then to slip into our jimjams for the night. By the time we've finished, in approximately an hour, I expect the children's presents to be back here. I don't care how you do it, but you're not driving, nor are we. Sort it out and sort it out quickly, otherwise the three of you will be spending the night outside.' They march past us like a battalion of Cybermen. At least Gillian throws me an apologetic smile and mimes the word "sorry" as she passes by. We watch in silence as they disappear upstairs.

'Well, Stanley, here's another fine mess you got me into,' Geordie sighs.

7: Hark! The Herald Angels Sing

The three of us retire to the safety of the recording studio with a plate of sausage rolls. I splash whisky into three glasses and hand them out.

'I'm running out of ideas, fast,' I say, as I light a cigarette and sip on my drink. Geordie is busy hoeing into the rolls at a rate of knots.

'Not a problem,' he mumbles as bits of pastry fall to the floor. 'Give Lord Cumberfutch a call and explain the situation. He may have sobered up by now. I'm sure he'll drive the car over.'

'Maybe. I don't even have his number. I'll have to look it up.'

'It will be on his business card he handed you,' he says as he rams another roll into his mouth.

I'm puzzled. 'I can't remember him handing me a business card?' I say.

'Yes, he did. When we were in the study. It was not long after you invited him for Christmas dinner tomorrow,' he replies nonchalantly.

'I WHAT?'

'Invited him for dinner.' A hazy, unwelcome recollection drifts through my mind. I shoot a glance at Robbo.

'It's true. You and him were like best pals, backslapping and complimenting each other,' Robbo adds.

'And what did he say? I'm praying for the right answer.

'He declined.'

'Phew! Thank God for that.'

71

'At first,' Robbo continues. 'But you were so insistent, he finally agreed. "My home is your home, Stanley. Meet our lovely children and beautiful wives, Stanley. You'll be welcomed with open arms, Lord Cumberfutch. The more the merrier. No, of course my wife won't mind, she'll be delighted." You were like two long-lost army buddies.' My heart has dropped into my bowels.

'I'm a walking dead man. What's Fiona going to say when I tell her I've invited a complete stranger to our family dinner?'

'Use your imagination,' Geordie says, appearing oblivious to my internal anguish. 'And it won't be pretty. Anyway, don't worry about that now. We have more pressing matters, such as the presents in the boot of your bloody car.' I search my trouser pockets and pull out his Lordship's business card. I quickly tap in the numbers on my phone.

'Hello, Stanley Cumberfutch speaking.'

'Stanley, it's Will Harding, here.'

'Will Harding?'

'Yes. I was round at your gaff this afternoon, drinking brandy with you. The Christmas tree saga?'

'Ah! Will, how are you? Did you get home safely?'

'Yes, thanks. We have a bit of a dilemma, though. The car we left in your driveway has all the kids' presents in the boot.'

'Oh, I see your problem. I'd love to help you out and drop the car off for you, but regrettably I got rather a taste for the peach brandy and I'd be way over the limit. Are any of you sober enough to drive out here?'

'No. We would have been sober by now if it hadn't been for someone's insistence we have a refreshing ale to gird our loins. Unfortunately, that opened the floodgates again,' I explain, glaring at Geordie, who has devoured the last of the sausage rolls. Greedy get!

'Hmm... let me think. Of course! I have a solution. I'll get Jitters to drive the car over then he can get a taxi back.'

'Brilliant! Thanks, Stanley. You may have saved the day.'

'My pleasure.'

'I'll text through my address. Bye.' I hang up.

'What did he say?' Robbo asks as he replenishes our glasses.

'He's sending Jitters over with the car. Will this day never end? Surely we've got to be in the clear now?'

'You know your problem, Billy Boy. You worry too much. Always have done. You need to relax, then good things will happen to you.'

'He's right,' Robbo agrees. 'Chill and go with the flow. The universe will sort things out. It always does.' I glance around the studio looking for a suitable weapon of choice that can slay two men with one blow.

*****

I welcome Jitters into the house and guide him through to the dining room where Robbo and Geordie are sitting. He looks frozen to the marrow.

'Can I get you a hot drink, Jitters?'

'Thank you, sir. A hot cup of sweet tea would hit the spot.'

'No problem. You pull your chair up to the fire and get a warm.'

'You can fix a brew for me and Robbo, while you're out there, Bill,' Geordie shouts. Hmm... I wonder if I've got any cyanide in the cupboard?

I place four cups of hot tea onto the tray and head back into the dining room.

'Here we go.' I hand Jitters his tea which he accepts gratefully. 'The taxi should be here in about fifteen minutes.' He nods as his shaking hand lifts the cup to his lips. Geordie leans into the side of him.

73

'Say, Jitters, would you care for a shot of whiskey in your tea? Warm the cockles—eh?'

Jitters smiles. 'Oh, if you don't mind, sir. I do usually have a hot toddy on a night.'

'That's the spirit,' says Geordie as he grabs a bottle of single malt off the top of the piano. He pours a very generous shot into Jitters tea then follows suit with the rest of the cups. He sits back down and takes a satisfying slurp on his tea. 'Ah, just the ticket.'

We spend the next ten minutes finding out about Jitters. It turns out he's a keen horticulturist and an expert in the propagation of orchids. He has a greenhouse behind Cumberfutch Manor. He exhibits at the Royal Horticultural Show every year.

If someone had told me this morning, that by the end of the day, I'd be sharing a hot toddy with Lord Cumberfutch's butler, discussing orchids, I'd have said they were crazy. Life is sometimes strange.

Footsteps on the stairs has us exchanging nervous glances with each other. The door bursts open and Jackie marches in. She glares at us malevolently until her eyes rest on Jitters and her frown softens.

'Jackie, let me introduce you to Jitters, Lord Cumberfutch's butler. Jitters, this is my loving, adorable, and may I say, stunning wife,' says Geordie.

'Cut the crap,' she says to him before turning to Jitters. 'Pleased to meet you, Jitters.'

'Ma'am,' he nods, 'likewise.'

She turns to Geordie. 'Can I take it the children's presents are now safely home?' she asks, coldly.

'Of course, pet. Just another spot fire that me and the boys have safely put out.' She grabs a pair of hair straighteners off the sideboard and turns to him.

'A spot fire started by you and the boys,' she remarks. 'Little boys really shouldn't play with matches. They may get their fingers burnt.' Ouch! Geordie laughs nervously. As she heads towards the door, she stops and peers over the cups on the table. Geordie visibly freezes.

'It's only tea, sweetheart,' he says. Her eyes narrow as they silently swing around the table, eyeballing each one of us in turn.

'Hmm…' she says before disappearing out of the door. We let out an almighty sigh of relief.

Geordie grins. 'Women, eh? They can be so gullible. I'm the master of subterfuge,' he whispers, puffing out his chest.

'Oh, and Geordie?' Jackie's voice booms from the stairs.

He coughs, then swallows. 'Ye... yes, dear?'

'If I find out you've laced your tea with whiskey you know what's going to happen to you, don't you?' His hands involuntary fall over his testicles.

'I'm hurt at the very suggestion. You know, there needs to be trust and honesty in a relationship,' he calls back, before swigging his tea down in one go, indicating for me and Robbo to follow suit. There's a beep-beep that breaks the tension.

'That'll be the taxi,' I say.

'Robbo, take the cups into the kitchen and give them a good wash and rinse out,' mouths Geordie, accompanied by hand gestures. I escort Jitters to the front door and out into the cold, sharp night. I bob my head down to speak with the taxi driver.

'How much to Cumberfutch Manor?'

'Double time tonight, so about forty quid,' he replies. I feel for my wallet but don't have it. I turn to Geordie, who is sauntering down the path.

'Oi, Geordie, give me your wallet.'

'What for?'

'Never mind what for. Just pass me it.' He reluctantly relinquishes his wallet as if I'd asked him to hand over his firstborn to King Herod. I pull a fifty from the wallet and push it into the driver's hand. 'Keep the change and merry Christmas.'

'Thanks a lot. And a merry Christmas to you too.' I grab another fifty and pass it to Jitters, who is fastening his seatbelt in the back. 'Thanks, Jitters, we really appreciate it. Here, take this.'

'Thank you, sir. There really is no need.'

'Yes, there is. You've gone to a lot of trouble for us.'

'Okay, well that's very generous of you, sir,' he says as he eagerly stuffs the note into his pocket.

'Aye, it's easy to be generous with someone else's money,' Geordie grumbles in the background. I slam the car door shut and wish Jitters a merry Christmas as the car takes off. I hand the wallet back to Geordie as Robbo joins us outside.

'We best get these kids out of the bath and into their pyjamas,' says Robbo. Geordie looks at his watch.

'Nearly nine. Another thirty minutes and I better get into my Santa outfit,' he says.

'I've been meaning to ask you about that,' I start. 'What's the go again?'

'It's to make sure the kids go to sleep. I stand outside your bedroom window and gaze into a crystal ball which tells me all the kids are still awake. I then say in a loud voice that I'll return later when they're tucked up in bed and sound asleep. I've also got another few tricks up my sleeve. It'll be a wheeze!'

'It sounds like a bad idea to me. Won't that get them more excited?' Geordie laughs and pats me on the shoulder in a patronising manner.

76

'Billy Boy, you have a lot of good points… well, some, but when it comes to reverse psychology, leave it to the experts. You need to think like a child. I've been practising and have it down pat.'

'Thinking like a child?' Robbo queries.

'No, I have the Santa routine down pat. I even have sleigh bells and a big white sack that's full of polystyrene. The crystal ball is amazing. Wait until you see it, and hear it,' he guffaws.

'I hate to rain on your parade, but I see one teeny weeny fly in the ointment.'

'Here we go, Billy the naysayer. Go on then, what is it?'

'Santa Claus is universally depicted as a short fat bloke. Don't you think the kids will be a tad suspicious when a six-and-a-half foot bean pole materialises before their eyes. Robbo would have been a better choice to play the part,' I add.

'Oi, what's that supposed to mean?' says Robbo, looking puzzled and annoyed.

'Don't worry, Bill. It'll be dark. The kids are upstairs. They'll be too far away to notice. Anyway, just in case, I have a contingency plan.' He gropes around in his jacket and pulls out a small digital recorder and remote control. 'I've recorded myself snoring and saying a few words about shutting the bedroom door.'

'I'm intrigued, Inspector Gadget. Pray continue.'

'Jackie will stuff pillows under our blankets to make it look like I'm in bed. The recorder will be placed inside the drawer of the bedside cabinet. If the kids do think it's me dressed as Santa, you're to say that I'm asleep in bed. They'll no doubt all run to my bedroom to check. When they open the door, they'll notice a body shape under the blankets. Then, you press the remote and my snoring starts for a few seconds, followed by the pre-recorded message, telling them to shut the door. You see? You've got to think like a child thinks. Trust me Bill, I have a highly tuned sixth sense for these things. It will run like clockwork.' I shoot a glance at Robbo who raises one crooked eyebrow at me.

.

8: Santa Claus Is Coming To Town

The children and most of the adults are sitting in the living room watching The Polar Express. Flaky *is* in bed and Geordie is pretending to be in bed, whereas in reality, he's in the recording studio donning his Santa outfit. It's 9:30 pm and the little ones are getting sleepy. I figure this would be the perfect time to get them tucked in for the night—apparently not. The Santa Claus pantomime must play out.

There's a buzzing sound as Jackie stares at her mobile phone. The adults exchange glances. Jackie smiles and gives a surreptitious thumbs up. It looks like operation "Santa Shambles" is about to be launched. Another minute passes by.

'Wait! What's that sound I can hear?' Jackie declares in a hushed whisper. All the kids wearily turn to her.

'What sound?' Wallace asks.

'That sound,' continues Jackie. 'I do believe it could be sleigh bells. Let me mute the TV.' The little ones are suddenly wide eyed. 'There! Did you hear it that time?' There was indeed the discernible sound of a sleigh bell in the distance. The kids rush to the window and peer out into the dark night.

'It could be Santa Claus!' Wallace says scrunching up his eyes.

'But we're not in bed and Santa only comes once everyone's asleep,' Mary says with a troubled expression.

'Ah, that's the thing,' begins Fiona. 'Santa Claus can tell if all the little boys and girls are asleep. If they are, then he delivers their presents.'

'But what if they're not asleep?' Katrina says, appearing concerned.

'He goes to another house where the girls and boys are asleep and leave their presents. Then he'll come back once you *are* asleep,' explains Fiona. Little Robert seems perturbed by the statement.

'How does he know if we're asleep, though?'

'He has a magic crystal ball that he looks into,' Jackie says, patently enjoying the charade.

'Wait!' Wallace exclaims as his head bobs around behind the curtains. 'I can see someone at the very bottom of the garden and they're heading this way.'

'Quick!' shouts Fiona, 'Let's run upstairs and watch from the bedroom window. We'll be able to get a better view from there.' A cacophony of squeals and shrieks ring out as five excited children run hell for leather through the doorway and thunder up the stairs. The adults quickly follow.

Mustered in the bedroom, everyone is staring out of the window. The sleigh bell echoes out again. The kids giggle and squeeze each other. I'm standing next to Robbo and Jackie. She leans in and whispers in my ear.

'It's going amazingly well, don't you think?' she states, in an innocent, naive manner.

'Early doors,' I say. 'Give it time.' She slaps me playfully on the arm.

'Oh, ye of little faith. "You know who" has been working on this performance for weeks. He's told me he's got it down pat.'

'Really? I guess it should run like clockwork, then.'

She giggles. 'That's what he says.'

'Does he indeed.' She doesn't know her husband as well as I do.

'Ho, ho, ho, ho, ho,' a voice explodes from the garden below. Slowly, a colossal figure comes into view, dressed in a red coat and hat, sporting a long white beard and bearing a bulging sack slung over his shoulder.

'It's him, it's him,' the children whisper excitedly as they dance around clutching each other.

'Ho, ho, ho, ho, ho, ho,' comes the voice again. 'Yo, ho, ho, and a bottle of rum.'

'I think he may have deviated from the script slightly,' I murmur to Robbo.

'Let's hope he doesn't mention fifteen men on a dead man's chest, otherwise this whole thing could go tits up sooner than we predicted.'

'That looks like Uncle Geordie,' comments Mary, troubled by the peculiar proceedings.

'No, it can't be. I saw Uncle Geordie earlier, and he said he was going for a lie down as he was feeling tired,' I reassure them.

'I don't believe you,' challenges Wallace.

'Go see for yourself,' I reply. They all turn tail and hurtle down the corridor to Geordie's and Jackie's bedroom. I rush after them, ready to make my cameo appearance.

'Wait, kids. Open the door gently and quietly. You know how grumpy Uncle Geordie can be if you wake him up.' They nod their heads. Little Katrina tugs on the handle and the door slowly creaks open. They all poke their heads inside to have a gawp. There's a soft yellow light shining from a corner lamp which casts a shadow over the bed. The pillows are expertly arranged to highlight the figure of a tall human frame beneath the blankets. I've got to admit, it does look convincing. I push my hand into my pocket and press the "play" button on the remote control. The sound of gentle snoring fills the room.

'That's dad!' exclaims Robert. 'That's how he snores!'

'Wallace, Robert, daddy's taking a little catnap. Can you please close the door? Good boys,' states Geordie's disembodied sleepy voice. The kids stare goggle-eyed at each other.

'That means it must be the real Santa in the garden!' whispers Wallace. The kids race back to my bedroom and pack in tightly around the window to gain the best vantage point. Santa is about to mount the steps which lead to the patio. As he gets halfway up, the high-powered security lighting is triggered. It blazes down into Santa's eyes, which I assume have become accustomed to the dark. He squints for a moment, temporarily blinded, before losing his footing in the snow. It's a graceful fall off the edge of the steps for such a big man. The landing, however, doesn't quite carry the same degree of elegance.

'Ah! Jesus! My bastard knee!' His words indicate to me he may have landed on the upturned garden rake, which, if memory serves me correctly, was last seen in that vicinity. As he rises gingerly to his feet, he unwittingly releases a long, high-pitched and painful sounding fart. It's so strident, it startles the children, who visibly flinch.

'Haha! Santa farted!' Wallace cries.

'Did Santa swear?' Katrina asks, staring dolefully at Gillian.

'He said the "B" word,' Mary complains, who has now fallen into a heavy pouting mode, not unlike her mother, when things don't seem quite right. She's too young to appreciate Greek tragedies. 'He's naughty.'

'And he said Jesus,' Katrina points out.

'I think he said Jesus because it's the night baby Jesus was born,' Julie explains, clutching at invisible straws.

'What about the fart?' Wallace queries.

'That was an owl,' Fiona intervenes. 'There is a species of owl that has a call very similar to a rude noise. Isn't that right, Will?'

'Yes, it's called the Windy Owl, native to these parts.' Santa is still vigorously rubbing at his right knee. It's too early to conclusively say if the wheels have fallen off this particular bus, but they are looking decidedly wobbly.

Santa navigates the snow-covered steps again, a little slower this time. He emerges onto the patio breathing heavily. A few moments pass as he regains his composure.

'Ho, ho, ho, ho,' he cries again, this time with a tad less enthusiasm than the first time around. The women are looking on in nervous anticipation, whereas Robbo and I are looking on in gleeful expectation. Santa now has a good old scratch of his ballsack before stroking his beard thoughtfully.

'Santa scratched his balls!' Wallace yells in obvious delight. Fiona closes her eyes and shakes her head.

'Wallace!' Jackie scolds. 'Don't be rude!'

'It's true, it's true! He scratched his knackersack!'

Santa continues. 'Now, let me see, which little girls and boys live here? Ah yes, we have Wallace, Mary, Katrina and Sally. Hmm…I wonder if they're all fast asleep in their beds yet?'

'What about me?' Robert wails. 'He didn't say my name,' he sobs. Jackie picks him up in her arms to comfort him.

'That means you won't get any presents, haha!' his brother teases, which results in an increase in the volume and intensity of Robert's wailing.

'Of course, he'll get presents!' Jackie shouts. She's beginning to look a little flushed. 'Everyone will get presents. Santa forgot your name, that's all. Think of how many names he's got to remember from all around the world. Even Santa can forget sometimes. It doesn't mean you won't get your presents.' Imagine Santa forgetting his own son's name… what a klutz.

'Ho, ho, ho, hum. I'll check my magic crystal ball to see if they're asleep. If not, I shall return later from hither and yon to check again. Now, where did I put my crystal ball?'

'Where's Hither and Yon?' Katrina asks, staring at her mother.

'Erm, Hither and Yon are places at the North Pole,' Gillian replies. I glance down at Mary, who is trying hard to hold back the tears.

'What's the matter, Mary?' Fiona asks.

'I don't like Santa. I don't want him in our house. He swears, he makes rude noises, and he's too big. He's like a mountain. I'm scared.'

'Don't be silly, dear. Santa's a kind, gentle man. There's no need to be scared.' Mary doesn't look convinced, obviously a good judge of character. Katrina takes Mary's hand and gives it a gentle squeeze.

'Don't be scared, Mary, I'll save you from that nasty Santa.' Hmm... those wheels are becoming a definite health and safety issue.

Santa rummages about in his sack and retrieves a large white orb, which emits a silky light. I've got to say, it's pretty impressive. Blue milky clouds swirl around inside the ball. He holds it out in front of him in dramatic fashion, as if he's chief wizard at some pagan slaughter ritual. Silence falls over the bedroom as mouths gape and eyeballs bulge, and not just from the kids.

'Oh, mysterious, magic, crystal ball, I have but one question for you.'

'Go ahead, Santa and pose thy question,' the ball replies, in a deep ominous growl, which has been recorded with a ton of echo. I'm not sure which moron did the voiceover for the crystal ball, (although, I could hazard a guess) but he appears to have forgotten his intended audience. If it had been designed for a gothic horror film, where the crystal ball represents Beelzebub, then he'd have been bang on the money. However, as his listeners are five, innocent, overtired children, he seems to have misread the brief.

'Are all the little boys and girls in this dark abode fast asleep?'

'I hear thy question, oh powerful one, give me a moment.' Santa sweeps one hand around the nefarious globe, much akin to an ancient druid bringing forth evil spirits from the underworld. The kids are frozen rigid to the spot. In my experience, the only time children of this age keep still is when they're paralysed by fear.

'Oh, my word,' murmurs Julia as she clamps her hand over her mouth. 'It can only get better,' she mumbles. I don't have the heart to break the news to her.

'Hear me! Hear me! Hear me!' booms the orb.

'Eh up, sounds like there's a town crier on the loose,' Robbo drawls.

'I see four, erm, five faces. Little faces of boys and girls. Two boys, two girls… no, three girls,' says the all-knowing orb, apparently confused by how many children are residing in the dark abode.

'And tell me, oh wise one, are they unconscious yet?' Santa asks.

'Christ,' whispers Jackie, 'he sounds like a paedophile with a pocket full of Rohypnol.' There seems to be a glitch in proceedings as both Santa and the orb fall silent. The seconds tick.

'I repeat again, oh wise one, are the children unconscious yet?'

'You shall come hither and yon again, later!' cries the orb.

'Pardon?' Santa replies.

'The children are yet to sleep.'

'Then what am I to do, oh great wise orb?'

'Thou shall return when they sleep, under the cover of darkness. You shall creep into their dark abode and perform your rituals, as it is written.'

'Thank you most sagacious one. I shall return one last time to perform my deed. Hail thee, hail thee, hail thee!'

This could have been Geordie's *finest* hour. Alas, I fear it may be his final hour. He pulls the globe in closer until it's directly under his chin.

'Ooh, that's not a good look,' Robbo whispers. The light from the orb casts dark menacing shadows over Santa's face, highlighting a great big hooter and numerous facial scars. The scene is utterly terrifying. Is that Freddy Krueger or Father Christmas standing in the shadows below us? He stares up at the bedroom window and smiles, but due to the illumination, it comes across as a sinister grimace loaded with evil intent. To add a nice macabre twist, he's removed his false front tooth. The children are slapped awake from their living nightmare. There's an eruption of screams and shrieks.

'Quick, everybody! Hide!' Wallace yells, completely terrified. He sprints from the room, as the little ones chase after him wailing, crying, screaming.

'You can hide under the bed with me,' Katrina whispers with a petrified look on her face as she drags a sobbing Mary and Sally along behind her.

I believe Jackie is experiencing a rapid onrush of emotions. Humiliation, shame and embarrassment seem to be etched onto her reddening face. It doesn't last long though, maybe a second or two before a new passion announces itself—I believe it's called rage. She marches out of the room as the other women chase after their distraught offspring, leaving me and Robbo alone to take up front row seats.

'You've got to hand it to him, he certainly brought the house down,' I say.

'Indeed. The most masterful display of incompetence I've ever witnessed. You can't develop talent like that, you have to be born with it. He had everything down pat. His ability to think like a child was dazzling. Riveting viewing, and it's not over yet. There's still the final scene to come.'

'Ah yes, of course. Does our hero save the day, slay the monster and ride off into the sunset with his one true love?'

'Possibly… although I think this particular film might have a different ending. I'm not sure it's a "happy ever after," type of movie.'

'Yeah, I get a similar impression. Art house horror films, eh? They're so unpredictable.'

Outside, Santa is still holding the globe aloft, oblivious to the devastation and carnage he's wreaked inside.

'Ho, ho, ho!' he continues. 'And what have we here?' he says, glancing at the back door, with a surprised expression. 'Well, well, well, it appears to be a human lady woman…'

'Did he just say, human lady woman?' Robbo grins.

I nod. 'A very enraged and wrathful human lady woman.'

'Hell hath no fury…'

'Like a Jackie scorned.' I push open the windows. 'I wouldn't miss this for the world. I wish we'd brought popcorn.' We both stick our heads outside and stare down at the winter wonderland which could shortly become a bloodbath. Jackie marches straight up to Geordie, grabs his beard and pulls it sharply down.

'That elastic has some stretch to it,' Robbo comments.

'It certainly does. Right down to his knees. Who'd have thought?' She releases the beard. It catapults back up towards Geordie's face at a velocity that questions the laws of physics. The elastic is rudely brought to a halt by the soft tender flesh under his chin. The resulting cracking sound echoes out across the dark, barren landscape. To add to the theatre, a distant bird, which I assume was happily sleeping a second before, lets out a piercing squawk. Santa's head snaps back with such violence, I half expect to see his oversized noggin fall to the ground. Alas, only his red bonnet flutters to the soft snow below.

'Sweet merciful shite!' the man in red, roars.

'Santa didn't see that one coming, did he?' Robbo notes.

'No. You'd have thought his crystal ball might have given him some warning.'

'Or his highly tuned sixth sense.'

'Jesus H Christ and pockets of blood, woman!' Jackie follows up with an almighty kick to his shin. As Santa bends double, she grabs the crystal ball, which he's desperately been clinging onto as though he'd found the lost ark, and smashes it over his head.

'Ouch! Poor old Santa,' Robbo chuckles.

'What the hell do you think you were doing?' Jackie yells. 'You've traumatised the children! You were supposed to be playing Father Christmas. You looked more like a mass child murderer on the prowl. We could have dug up Bela Lugosi and dressed him in a Santa costume, and he'd have been less terrifying than you! Get inside now! You can explain to the kids it was you, joking around, otherwise we'll never get them to sleep. You've scarred them for life, you blundering, cack-handed, clodhopping dinglebat!' She turns and marches back inside.

'Wow! What a finale,' I murmur. 'I wonder if there'll be an encore?'

'It was one of those films you wished would never end.' Robbo leans out of the window. 'Ho, ho, ho and a merry Christmas to you Santa Claus,' he shouts, waving at him. Geordie stops rubbing his shin for a moment and glares up at our two smirking faces. He gives us the two-fingered salute with a certain amount of gusto.

'Well done, Santa. It ran like clockwork. Hey, I've got a message from Rudolph. He wants to know whether he should start the engines now or wait until you've finished your glass of sherry that's waiting for you on the fireplace?'

'Why don't you two go and f...' I pull the windows shut.

'Sublime.'

'Ridiculous.'

'Breath-taking.'

'Mind blowing.'

'After the fraught and fractious day we've had, that little twilight performance has quite buoyed my spirits,' I say.

'Unlike the spirits of our children and long-suffering wives.'

'Hmm... indeed. Okay, time to weave our magic, Robbo, before the hobgoblin dinglebat comes clomping up the stairs to stir it all up again.'

9: Good King Wenceslas

The grand masterplan failed miserably. By staging the Faustian play the previous night, it was assumed it would delay the children from sleeping by about half an hour. It was hoped this delay would stop them from rising too early in the morning. It took us a good hour to calm them down and reassure them it was Uncle Geordie's idea of a silly joke and Santa wasn't really evil. They finally fell asleep just after 11 pm.

Some adults foolishly believed the kids would sleep until about seven or even eight o'clock the next day. Highly optimistic, in my opinion.

At 5 am we were all dragged from our beds by five adorable but overly excited children. At least they appeared to have forgotten about the dark satanic rituals that occurred on the eve of Christmas.

The women put up a good show. Although tired and weary, they were determined to savour the moment as presents were ripped open amid shrieks of delight and excited chatter.

For the men it was a slightly different scenario that played out. Groggy and hungover, the four of us sat on one couch together. With strained, false smiles we endured two hours of deafening mayhem. Flaky was, by far, in the worst state, so there's always an upside to every situation. He wore an icepack on his head and every time a child shouted or screeched with laughter, I could see him wince and close his eyes. At one point I thought he'd gone into cardiac arrest, but all he'd done was move his head too quickly.

We helped the children move their toys to their bedrooms where we assembled Scalextric and dolls' houses, fitted batteries to various gadgets, unpacked Lego, and read stories from a multitude of shiny new books. Once they were all settled I went to the bathroom and dropped two electrolyte tablets into a large glass of water then slunk off back to my bedroom hoping to sneak in another hour or two of hallowed sleep. I'm not sure what the other three did, but I assume, if they had any sense, they'd follow a similar plan.

*****

A loud popping noise wakes me with a start. *What the hell was that?* My heart is pounding. I glance at the clock—9:17 am. Silence. I drift back off to sleep. I wake again, twenty minutes later, by cackling laughter and shrill voices. I groggily rouse myself and sit up in bed. *Hmm… sounds like the girls are well into their first bottle of champers.* I stagger to the shower and luxuriate under warm water for a good fifteen minutes until I feel human once more. I dry, quickly dress and head downstairs. The kitchen is a hive of activity, so I bypass it and head straight to the dining room. Robbo and Geordie are sitting around the table munching on bacon and egg sandwiches. In the centre of the table is a jug of iced water, a plunger of freshly brewed coffee, a packet of paracetamol and a plate that still holds two bacon and egg rolls.

'Went for a crafty sleep, did you, Bill?' Geordie grins.

'Yeah, I needed it,' I say as I pour myself a coffee.

'Yeah, me and Geordie too,' Robbo says as egg yolk slides down his chin.

I take two large gulps of coffee. 'Oh, yes. That is nectar.' I grab a roll and tuck into it with voracious relish.

'How are the girls?' I say, after I devour the first mouthful.

'Which ones? The big ones or the little ones?' Geordie asks.

'The big ones.'

'They're good now they've cracked their first bottle of sparkling. I also turned on the Geordie charm offensive. Never fails. I got the cold shoulder initially, but you know me, I'm not one to be deterred. Now I've got them eating out of the palm of my hand.'

'Nothing to do with the alcohol that kicked in about twenty minutes ago?' Robbo says through a mouthful of egg.

'All's well that ends well.' I say.

'Aye, all good,' says Geordie. 'If you ever need someone to turn a situation around then I'm your man. Although, I lay the blame for yesterday's catalogue of disasters firmly at *your door*.'

'Of course, you do.'

'If you'd listened to your wife and got the tree earlier, we wouldn't have ended up at Cumberfutch Manor getting slaughtered.'

'And the midnight performance of Sweeney Todd meets Hannibal Lecter?' I say as I finish the roll and drain my coffee cup. For a man who totally stuffed up Christmas Eve, he appears unperturbed.

'A mere hiccup in the rich tapestry of life,' he replies nonchalantly as I eye the last roll on the plate.

'You have it, Bill. I've already had four,' Geordie says, patting his stomach with satisfaction. 'I'm starting to come good. I reckon a hair of the dog and I'll be firing on all cylinders again.' I take the last roll and tuck in. He grabs a toothpick, leans back in his chair and scratches at his teeth. I laugh. 'What's funny?' he asks.

'That large red welt under your chin. It's formed into a perfect arc. It looks like someone's tried to slash your throat.' He grimaces as he touches it with his thumb.

'That woman! She flies off the handle at the slightest thing.'

'The slightest thing?' says Robbo with an element of surprise. 'Even I had nightmares.'

'Hmm… it was a good idea in theory.'

'Yeah, it was the delivery that let it down.'

'I may have over thought it.'

'I think you may have overacted it. You could go on the road with that stage play. I can see your name in lights now. Geordie Kincaid in the one man show—Appointment with Fear!' Geordie throws Robbo a disparaging glance.

'Where's Flaky?' I ask.

'In the living room laid out on the couch with an ice pack on his head. Weak as piss. He looks like shit on a stick,' Geordie replies. He flicks the toothpick into the open fire as he spies a balloon on the floor. He bends over and picks it up. A smile drifts across his face. I finish my second roll and refill my coffee cup. Geordie gets to his feet.

'Hey, follow me,' he says as he grabs a drawing pin from the sideboard. We follow him out of the dining room, cross the hall, and tiptoe quietly into the living room. We are greeted with soft steady snores. Geordie places the balloon at the side of Flaky's head, then jabs the pin into it. Up until now I hadn't believed in levitation.

'Holy thunder!' Flaky screeches as he bounces off the couch and onto the floor. 'You great big blundering oaf! Why would you do such a thing?' he yells.

'That's payback for last night,' Geordie replies. 'You got away with blue murder, slinking off to bed early, leaving us three to clean up your mess.'

'I had a hangover. I wasn't feeling very well!'

'You know what your trouble is?'

'No! But I'm sure I'm going to get the philosophical wisdom of Geordie.'

'You don't drink enough.'

'Oh, I see. I drink too much and get a chronic hangover and the solution is to drink more?'

'Aye, exactly right. You need to condition the body. It's like training to be an athlete.'

'Alcohol is a poison.'

'You weren't saying that yesterday.'

'We all make mistakes. That is one mistake that will not be made again. I'm never going to touch another drop.'

'Ah,' Robbo says, 'spoken like a true alcoholic.'

'Unlike you three, I am not a bloody alcoholic!' It's hard to know definitively, but I don't think Flaky is in the best of moods.

'I'm going to get a shower and freshen up,' Robbo says as he leaves the room.

'Yes, me too,' Flaky says.

Geordie and I return to the dining room and idly chitchat about some songs we've been working on. A few minutes pass when the door opens, and Fiona sticks her head inside.

'Hey, Will, where did you put the champagne?'

'There was one bottle in the fridge.'

'Yes, I know, we've drunk that one, but I asked you to get a case.'

'Yes, you did, but Geordie said he'd take care of it, so I didn't bother.' Fiona is joined by Jackie, Gillian and Julie. All eyes turn to Geordie.

'Geordie, where have you put the champagne?' demands his wife. 'Please don't tell me you've left it in the boot of the car?'

'Don't worry,' says Julie, 'it was bitterly cold last night so it will be nicely chilled.'

94

'Do us a favour, Will,' says Fiona. 'Can you grab them from the car?'

'Yes, sure,' I reply.

'Ahem,' Geordie says as he clears his throat. The four women stop dead in their tracks. Everyone knows what the Geordie "Ahem" means.

'Ahem, what?' Jackie asks, her eyes narrowing to slits.

'They're in the pantry,' he mumbles with a reticence I know only too well. 'The erm, the pantry at our house.'

'In Edinburgh!' Julie exclaims.

'Yes, that's where the house was the last time I looked.'

Jackie shakes her head in disbelief. 'My God! Just when you think it's safe to get back in the water. I told you four or five times not to forget the damned champagne. Great! I suppose you boys are all sorted for your own drinks? I bet you didn't leave them in the pantry?'

'No fear of that,' Geordie laughs before realising he's probably one more stupid comment away from the ICU. The women storm out. I turn to the oaf.

'You great big clot! I have them eating out of the palm of my hand, all's good, the Geordie charm offensive!'

'Hey, chill out, Billy Boy.'

'I was chilled out up until thirty seconds ago!' An angry silence enters the room for a few minutes, as Geordie looks suitably chastised.

'Hey, Bill, I have a little surprise for you. This will cheer you up.'

'I doubt it.'

'Guess what I've got stashed in my suitcase upstairs?'

'Twelve bottles of champagne?' I say. He leans forward and glances over his shoulder towards the door.

95

'No. Way better than that. I have a bottle of Glenfarclas whiskey. It's 40 years old… £550 per bottle. Perfect for Christmas time. This is only for you and me… right? No point giving it to Flaky or Robbo. They wouldn't know if it was petrol or paraffin,' he whispers. I'm suitably placated. 'Oh, and another thing?'

'What?'

'Not a word to Jackie or any of the girls, right? If she finds out I've spent £550 on a bottle of whiskey she'll string me up by my plums. Women… they don't appreciate the true value of things like we do.'

'Okay. I'll not say a word. We don't want any more domestics.'

'Good man.'

*****

Thirty minutes pass before Flaky reappears. Apart from his fresh smell and clean clothing, he doesn't look much better than when he left. He's turned a peculiar shade of green, not dissimilar to day old cabbage.

'What the hell is that jumper you're wearing?' Geordie laughs. He's wearing a florid yellow woollen number with a red bauble patterned on the front.

'I'll have you know my mother knitted this for me many moons ago,' he replies testily.

'If I had a jumper like that, I'd never wear it. You'll scare the bairns with that one,' he adds as he walks out of the door. 'I better see if I can win these women over again.' We can hear his voice as clear as day as he offers his services in the kitchen.

'Ladies, is there anything I can do to help out here? You know me, always willing and eager.'

'No thanks, Geordie,' begins Jackie. 'If we want to overcook the turkey, boil the Brussel sprouts to death, burn the gravy, poison the dog or burn the house down, then we'll give you a shout.' He re-enters the dining room looking chastened.

'Ah, the old Geordie charm, eh,' I smirk at him. The door is flung open as Robbo rushes in. The blood has drained from his face and his hands tremble violently.

'Delayed hangover?' Geordie asks. Robbo stares at him wild-eyed and shakes his head.

'No,' is his curt response.

'What's the problem?' I ask.

'Not good. In fact, terrible,' he spits the words out in staccato fashion, then puts his finger to his lips as he stares towards the kitchen. 'Shush,' he adds. I've not seen him in this state since we were on tour years ago and someone stole his entire stash of weed on day one. 'We need to talk somewhere private, right now!' he declares. 'The recording studio,' he whispers. We all head towards the door apart from Flaky, who flops his head onto the table.

'I'll give it a miss,' he whines, sorrowfully. Geordie grabs him by the scruff of the neck and yanks him to his feet.

'Oi, noggin, we're all in this together, right?'

'You don't understand... I just want to die. My head is being pummelled by jackhammers.'

'Smarten yourself up, man! That's defeatist talk. Don't let the enemy hear you say that. No matter how you truly feel, you must exude confidence and energy. Imagine you're a young spring lamb frolicking in the clover.'

'I feel like a lamb queuing up at the abattoir.' Geordie passes him three paracetamol and a glass of water.

'Take these, you big Jesse, and quit your snivelling.'

'I'll tell Fiona we're nipping out to the studio to listen to a couple of demos me and Geordie have been working on. We don't want to arouse suspicion,' I say as I head out of the door. Robbo and Geordie nod their approval. The kitchen is a hubbub of activity and despite the scarcity of Champagne, everyone appears in good spirits.

'Fiona, love, me and the boys are heading over to the studio for five minutes. I want to play Robbo and Flaky the latest track me and Geordie have been working on.'

'Oh, no! Come on, Will! It's Christmas Day! Today is about the kids and family and friends.'

'I promise, sweetheart, we'll be over there no longer than five minutes… ten… max.' She tilts her head, resigned to the fact.

'Okay. But if you're not back here in ten minutes then I'm coming for you!'

We traipse outside and navigate the huge drifts of snow which have fallen overnight. As we tackle the steps down into the garden, I call out.

'Hey, Geordie, watch the step!'

'Oh, very droll. What a comedian.' We enter the studio and shut the door behind us. The silence is a welcome relief from the chaotic nature of the house. Geordie makes a beeline for the bar fridge, retrieves four beers and hands them out. Flaky declines.

'I couldn't possibly,' he moans. Geordie twists the cap off and thrusts it into Flaky's chest.

'Drink it. I'm telling you, it will make you feel better. Not completely better, but it will get rid of the headache. Trust me.' Flaky eyes him suspiciously but takes the beer.

'The floor's yours, Robbo,' I say. He slumps into a chair, then takes a nervous glug of beer, his hands still shaking.

'It's the ring. It's gone,' he states like a man who has lost the will to live.

'What do you mean, gone?' I say.

'I mean bloody gone!' he snaps. 'It was in my coat pocket and it's not there anymore.'

'Are you sure? Have you checked all the pockets?' Flaky asks. Robbo gazes at him, sad, troubled.

'Yep. Ten times. I've turned the bedroom upside down. I've checked Geordie's car, top to bottom. I've lost it.'

'Okay, calm down,' I begin. 'Let's walk through this. When was the last time you saw it?'

'Yesterday, in Skipton, in the car.'

'And you definitely put it in your jacket pocket.'

'Yep. Definitely. I remember dropping it into the pocket on my righthand side.'

'You've always been careless with things,' Geordie sniffs. Robbo rounds on him.

'Excuse me, but this is all your bloody fault!' he yells.

'How do you work that one out?'

'When you threw me down that hill yesterday. That's the only place I could have lost it!'

'Don't blame me! Anyway, it serves you right for being ostentatious. £5000 for a bloody Christmas present. Who do you think you are—Aristotle Onassis?' Robbo sends his chair sprawling back and shakes his fist at Geordie.

'Another word and I swear I'm going to swing for you!'

'Aye, take your best shot, wee man. I'll let you have the first punch. Even things up,' Geordie scoffs not the slightest bit intimidated. Robbo picks his chair up and collapses into it.

'Can everyone calm down and put their thinking caps on?' I suggest.

'Aye, Bill's right. We're all getting a little overexcited. If anyone can come up with a plan to get you out of this shemozzle of your own making, then it's Bill.' There's a few seconds' calm as we sup our beer.

'Right,' I begin, 'Let's go through the scenario. You've lost a five-grand ring. That hurts. But there's another issue at hand.'

'Correct,' Robbo says, one step ahead of me. 'When we gather around the fireplace at 3 o'clock, each partner will exchange their gifts with one another. And I have nothing to give. It's total humiliation for Julie in front of her friends and the kids.' We fall silent.

'There's only one thing for it, Robbo. You're going to have to fess up to her and get it out in the open. For God's sake don't tell her how much you spent though. Tell her it was £300 or something. Tomorrow, you take her on a romantic trip to Skipton and buy a new one. Maybe take her out for lunch. She's a reasonable and easy-going woman, she'll understand,' I advise.

'Aye, that's true. If it were my wife, she'd be reaching for the carving knife. Count your blessings,' Geordie says, not helping the situation.

'You're right. That's all I can do,' Robbo murmurs, as his state of panic subsides, replaced by misery.'

'Come on everybody! Buck up. It's Christmas Day. We've got great food coming, music, a houseful of happy kids and happy… erm, a houseful of wives. The future belongs to us. We're going to make sure the rest of this holiday is one to remember,' I say, trying to sound positive.

'It's one to remember already,' Flaky moans, 'and we're only two days in.'

I hold my bottle out in front of me. 'Merry Christmas everybody and here's to better times ahead.' Smiles spread across their faces, followed by a few chuckles.

'Aye, to better times!' Geordie shouts. We clink bottles and force the beer down in one swift hit.

'Everything sorted,' I state as we head out of the studio. 'Oh no!' I drop to my haunches and hold my head in my hands. 'Shit the bed!'

'What's wrong, Will?' asks Flaky.

'Lord Cumberfutch, that's what. I haven't told Fiona we have an unexpected guest arriving and it's nearly one o'clock.'

'What time's he arriving?' Robbo asks.

'One o'clock,' I reply.

'Ring him and cancel,' Geordie says.

'He'll be turning up any minute. I can't cancel at this late stage. That would be rude. Damn it! I'll have to tell her right now.'

'The girls aren't going to be pleased with an unannounced visitor at this late stage,' Flaky remarks, stating the bleeding obvious.

'No, they're not. It'll be about as popular as a wet turd in a jacuzzi,' Geordie adds.

10: O' Come All Ye Faithful

The women are staring at me. No, they're not—they're glaring at me.

'You've invited who for dinner?' Fiona says.

'Lord Cumberfutch, you know, the guy we met yesterday.'

'And you decide to tell me one hour before we serve Christmas dinner?'

'It slipped my mind, what with all the excitement.'

'And when is he due?'

'About now.'

'They're unreal, aren't they?' Jackie scowls as she turns to her comrades in folded arms.

'He's a very nice man,' Flaky says, almost apologetically.

'Aye, he is a nice man, isn't he Robbo?' Geordie says.

'A very nice man.'

'He lost his wife last year, and his son a few years before that, in the Afghan War. I felt sorry for him and it is Christmas, you know, the time to lend a helping hand and all that,' I explain.

Fiona huffs. 'It's too late to do anything about it now. It's going to make things very awkward, sharing our family Christmas dinner with a complete stranger.'

'You'll get on fine with him. He's a very…'

'Nice man?' Julie offers.

'Yes, a very, ahem, nice man.' The sound of a car engine distracts us as we peer out of the kitchen window. A Bentley pulls up outside the front gate and Lord Cumberfutch steps out clutching a bouquet. He makes his way down the garden path and raps on the front door. Everyone stares at me.

'Are you going to let him in, or shall we all hide under the stairs and pretend we've gone out?' Fiona snipes. I open the door.

'Ah, Will, I hope you hadn't forgotten you'd invited me? I feel rather like an intruder.'

'Haha! No, not at all Lord Cumberfutch. We've been looking forward to your arrival all morning. Please come in and I'll introduce you to everyone.' He bangs his shoes on the step to shed the snow, then strides inside. 'You met the boys yesterday.'

'Merry Christmas, chaps,' he beams. They all offer him greetings in return.

'This is my lovely wife, Fiona,' I say, holding my arm out in her direction.

'Pleased to meet you, your Lordship,' she says, putting on her most welcoming smile.

'Oh, please, call me Stanley. No need to stand on ceremony.'

'Why should she call him Stanley?' Geordie whispers in my ear.

'Because that's his bloody name, you knobhead,' I reply through gritted teeth. Fiona takes over the introductions and as she announces each of her friends, Stanley takes their hand and kisses the back of it gently, whilst saying,

'What an honour and pleasure to meet you, my dear.'

'Likewise,' they all repeat.

'My oh my! What a group of radiant beauties.' He turns to me. 'I've got to say, I'm rather surprised.' I'm not sure I appreciate the comment.

'Surprised?'

'Yes, I'd say you boys are batting well outside of your crease.' The women laugh and make a few unnecessary comments. He hands the flowers to Fiona who blushes slightly. 'Righto chaps, I have a few gifts in the boot of my car. If you'd care to lend a hand.' Lord Cumberfutch heads to the door as we fall in behind him.

He opens the boot and lifts out a large box and places it into Geordie's arms.

'Twelve bottles of the finest Bollinger Champagne.' He extracts another box and dumps it into Flaky's hands. 'And twelve bottles of Rivata Casa Rossa, my favourite red and a bottle of brandy. I hope you like red?'

'I have been known to have a tipple, occasionally,' I reply.

'Huh, occasionally,' Flaky huffs. Lord Cumberfutch slams the boot shut and we turn to head back inside.

'Oh, wait. I have something I want you to see.' He opens the passenger door and scrabbles about in the glovebox. 'I went for a canter early this morning, over at Fallside Gap and I came across... now where is it? Ah, yes, here it is.' Clasped between his finger and thumb is a small ring box. Robbo grabs it from him and opens it up.

'Oh, you star, you bloody little star,' he exclaims as he hops from foot to foot. 'You've saved my bacon. I can't tell you what this means to me.' He grabs the Lord by the side of the ears and plants a big smacker on his forehead. Stanley looks bemused.

'I thought it may belong to one of you, as few people go to that neck of the woods, especially when there's been heavy falls. You were damn lucky, my fellow. It was resting on a large rock, with only a whisper of an edge sticking out. It was a miracle I spotted it at all.' We make our way back inside.

'Girls, good news—we have champagne!' The cheers are deafening.

*****

104

Flaky and Robbo are showing Stanley around the house and pointing out whose kids are whose. Meanwhile, me and Geordie have been collared in the hallway by Fiona.

'Will, Geordie, can you prepare the outside fire for this afternoon's sing song?'

'Where are you going to set it up? Geordie asks.

'Next to the Christmas tree.'

'Don't talk daft, man! You'll have the tree on fire.'

'Calm down. I have an old oil drum that I've made into a brazier. We may as well get it going now. It takes a while to heat up. I've plenty of dry wood in the shed. Come on grab your coat.' Before I can move Fiona grabs me by the elbow. She takes a furtive look around her and leans into me.

'You must find a gift for his Lordship,' she whispers.

'His Lordship?'

'Yes, his Lordship.'

'Listen to you two,' scoffs Geordie. 'You English are all the same. Give a man a title and you're doffing your caps and wringing your hands. Pathetic. You wouldnae find a Scot putting on airs and graces. We treat each man as we find them.' We ignore his comments.

'What sort of gift?'

'I don't know,' Fiona says. 'But it's going to be awkward when we're handing out the presents this afternoon and there's nothing for Lord Cumberfutch. He did bring expensive Champagne, red wine and brandy. It would be rude not to give him something in return. It doesn't have to be anything too flash. You know, just a little wrap up.' She turns to head back into the kitchen. 'Oh, and make sure it isn't anything inappropriate, I know what you're like. What you find funny, other people find crude and crass. Remember, you're dealing with nobility now.'

105

'Pfaff!' Geordie snorts. 'Nobility, indeed.'

I rub my chin trying to think of a suitable gift. 'What sort of gift do you give to a Lord?' I wonder aloud.

'Cornwall? North Yorkshire? Africa?'

'You're not helping, Geordie. Wait, I have it.' I stare at my big gormless friend.

'What? What? Why are you staring at me like that?' A few seconds elapse until my telepathic powers work their magic. 'Oh no, definitely not! Absolutely no way. You're the host, you find something for him, but he's not getting my bottle of Glenfarclas whiskey. Over my dead body.'

'Come on, Geordie, be nice. He's brought us a case of Bollinger, a case of Ryvita Casta… whatever, and a bottle of Napoleon Brandy. You wouldn't get much change out of a thousand quid for that lot.'

'No, please, Bill! I'm begging you, don't make me do this.' I fix him with a steely glare. He caves in and drops to his knees and burrows his face into his palms. 'No, no,' he wails, rocking back and forth. 'This cannae be happening. Oh Lord, why have you forsaken me? That's £550, £550…'

'What are you doing down there, you big lummox?' Jackie barks, as she once again materialises out of thin air. Geordie looks like a startled rabbit in the headlights. 'And what's £550?'

'Erm, nothing,' he stammers.

'It must be something. People don't fall to their knees and wail £550 for nothing.'

'It was, erm,' I begin, 'erm, we were totting up how much Lord Cumberfutch's gifts would have cost him.'

'Aye, that's right,' Geordie agrees, overly enthusiastic.

'Really?' Jackie replies. Her eyes narrow as they flit between me and her husband. 'And why are you on your knees?'

'It's the fall I took last night. My right knee gave way. I told you I'd damaged it, not that I got an ounce of sympathy out of you.'

'Is that so?' she replies, even more suspicious. 'Stand up man, you look ridiculous down there. Haven't you two got a job to do?' Geordie leaps to his feet.

'Aye, that's right. The fire. Come on Bill, we can't stand around here all day navel gazing. That's the problem with you, you'll do anything to get out of hard work.' We grab our coats and head towards the back door. Jackie calls out,

'Oh, and Geordie,'

'Yes, dearest?'

'I've got my eye on you—remember that.' We bustle each other out of the door and head straight to the studio to grab a calming beer.

*****

The Christmas dinner is magnificent; roast pork, roast turkey and a vast assortment of vegetables finished off with a rich plum pudding with rum sauce. Oh, and of course copious amounts of Champagne and red wine. Laughter rings out, crackers are pulled, and those annoying itchy paper hats are worn. The children make their way outside to play in the snow. The boys have built a sledge ramp in the garden. A gentle slope ideal for the younger ones. I've got to say, it has all been totally wonderful, and no mishaps! Everyone is in fine fettle and all grievances, whether false or justified, appear to have been banished.

Lord Cumberfutch raps the side of his wineglass with a spoon and rises to his feet. The room falls silent.

'Ahem, if I could have your attention please, ladies and gentlemen. I don't intend to make a fussy, dreary old speech today.'

'Hear, hear!' Geordie shouts. He's greeted with withering glares from the women and Flaky. Lord Cumberfutch chuckles and nods his head, then continues.

'I think it only fitting that I say a few words.' I stare at the faces around the table. The women seem quite smitten with his Lordship. He's dapper, refined, a wealth of knowledge, courteous and respectful. I'm not sure what they see in him, myself.

'You have welcomed me into your home with open arms and an air of generous hospitality that I can barely remember. It's been delightful to meet you all and your wonderful children who are an absolute credit to you. I've had some bleak times over the last few years, and I won't lower the mood by going into them here, suffice to say there were days when I didn't think I'd ever smile again, let alone laugh like I have done today or yesterday.' He stops and looks at me, Robbo, Flaky and Geordie. 'Yesterday, I met your husbands for the first time, and let's say we didn't get off to the best of starts.'

'Surprise, surprise,' Jackie comments accompanied by a matronly glare at the men.

'I had my prejudices about them, as I'm sure they had prejudices against me. How strange life is that a simple Christmas tree can bring people together from such divergent backgrounds. We can have titles, speak in different accents and have unique life experiences and yet, underneath, we are all human, one and the same.

We laugh, we cry. We bleed the same colour blood.' The girls sniff, even Flaky looks like he's welling up. 'I'd like to finish by saying, you have opened my eyes to life and what it can be, eyes that have been shut behind dark blinds for far too long. I thank each and every one of you and hope this is the beginning of a long and lasting friendship. The old adage says we can't choose our family, but we can choose our friends and friendship is what oils the wheels of life. Thank you.' Everyone erupts into applause, even Geordie, although he's not as ebullient as some of the others.

'Thank you, Stanley, I'm all choked up,' Fiona gushes.

'That was beautiful. So eloquent,' Gillian says.

'I'm truly touched,' Julie cries.

'You're right, Stanley, friendship is everything,' Jackie sniffs as she reaches out for Fiona's and Julie's hands.

'I think it's about time me and the boys cleared the table and tidied the kitchen,' I announce as I stack plates together. Geordie picks up the remnants of the turkey and heads towards the kitchen.

'Geordie?' Jackie calls out.

'Yes, dear?'

'Remember not to stack the cooked meats next to the raw meats. The last time you did that we all came down with salmonella for a week.'

'Of course, dear. I'm hardly likely to forget, not when you remind me so often.'

'Will?'

'Yes, Fiona?'

'Me and the girls and Stanley are going to retire to the living room. Once you've tidied the kitchen, we'll open the presents, yes?'

'Yep, good idea. We should be done in about thirty minutes.'

As we stack plates and cutlery into the dishwasher, I pull Geordie to one side.

'I need to ask you a favour,' I say. He stares down his long hooter at me, apprehensive, guarded.

'If you want more money, then you can forget it. You still owe me for the saw, the taxi driver and the fifty you slipped to Jitters, which by the way, you took the credit for.'

'No, it's not money.'

'Go on then, what is it?'

'Please, just for me, do not give the ironing board cover as a present to Jackie.'

He appears confused. 'Why not?' Robbo and Flaky both emit long, frustrated sighs.

'If you don't know the reason, then I'm not going to explain it to you. Please, promise me, you won't.' He looks thoughtful for a moment.

'I've explained before; me and Jackie have a deep understanding of each other. We're like two peas in a...'

'A pod, yes, I know. All the same.'

'Okay, Billy Boy. If it makes you happy, I won't.'

'Good. Good man.'

'I'll save it for her birthday.'

11: The Holly & The Ivy

The men are handed their presents first. Designer clothes, expensive watches, the latest and greatest mobile phones; boxsets of CDs from favourite artists, aftershave, underpants and of course, socks. All are opened with enthusiasm.

Next, the tables are turned, as the men hand their wives their gifts. Fiona and Gillian are delighted with their presents, the Gucci handbag for Fiona and a bracelet for Gillian. Flaky and I both receive adoring kisses from our spouses.

Robbo hands Julie her present. She peels back the wrapping and pulls the ring from the box. A chorus of "oohs" and "ah's" fill the room by the other women, as Julie gently sobs.

'Oh, Robbo, you shouldn't have. This must have cost a small fortune?' Robbo looks like the cat that got the cream. He smiles cockily at me and Geordie.

'You deserve it, my love, for putting up with me all year. It can't be easy. I'm man enough to realise that.' Geordie mumbles something and screws his nose up as though he's stood in something disgusting. 'What's the point of money if you don't spend it?' Robbo continues, gloating in his moment of shining glory.

'Noble sentiments, indeed,' I say. 'Don't you agree, Geordie?'

'Aye, very noble,' he sniffs.

Jackie is the last to open her gift. She puts on a stoic display as she holds the box of Milk Tray chocolates in the air.

'Oh, Geordie, how very retro of you! I haven't seen these since the 1970s. I didn't realise they still made them. And a Sportsgirl gift voucher for £50... it's been a while, maybe twenty years since I last visited Sportsgirl, but hey, I can reinvent myself as an eighteen-year-old. Thank you, darling!' Geordie leans forward for a kiss on the lips but receives a cold kiss to the cheek... not that he notices. Jackie throws a quick glance at the Gucci handbag, bracelet and ring, then purses her lips. She gets to her feet.

'What about that sing song around the Christmas tree?' There's a chorus of approval as people rise to their feet. Geordie glances over at me with a smarmy grin and one raised eyebrow as if he's just negotiated Armistice Day. He crosses one finger over the other, I assume to indicate two peas in a pod.

'Wait,' Fiona says. 'Will, haven't you forgotten something?'

'Oops, yes, sorry. Stanley, we have a little wrap up for you,' I reply as I walk towards the fireplace and grab the last remaining Christmas present.

'You shouldn't have!' exclaims Lord Cumberfutch. 'My gift has been sharing this day with you fine people.' Geordie rushes over to me, snatches the present from my hand and pushes me out of the way.

'No, you don't, sunshine,' he whispers asserting his authority. 'You're not going to steal the glory this time. This is my whisky and I'm going to get the kudos. Small recompense, but I'm not letting you get the plaudits.'

'Geordie, I don't think that's a good...' It's already too late as he strides confidently into the middle of the room.

'Stanley, please accept this gift from *me,* to you, on behalf of all of us... although it is from me... personally. Just a little something. A token of our appreciation.' Stanley takes the present graciously and shakes Geordie's hand.

'Thank you, Geordie. I'm not sure what to say.' Now his bloody Lordship is getting emotional. What's got into everybody?

'You don't have to say anything, Stanley. Not every act of selfless kindness and unmatched generosity needs to be acknowledged. Deep down we all know how you feel.' The big oaf is overplaying his hand. Stanley unwraps the paper and stares at the box. Momentarily stunned, he pulls his spectacles out of his jacket pocket and fumbles them onto his head.

'Oh, no! No, no! I cannot possibly accept this!' he proclaims.

'Oh, come, come, your Lordship,' Geordie says, sporting an arrogant leer. 'It's nought but a trifle, a soupcon, a mere flibberty gibbet in the grand scheme of things.' What the hell is he talking about? I glance around the room at the other faces. They appear as perplexed as me.

'No, really, I mean it. This is too much. I couldn't possibly accept it,' Stanley insists.

'Nonsense, Stanley. I would take it as a personal slight if you didn't accept it,' Geordie insists.

'This really is far too expensive,' he says. Jackie's ears prick up. A banana peel has come into view and it's lying about an inch away from Geordie's great big size twelve boots. Not that the plonker can see it.

'How expensive?' Jackie asks as she eyeballs her husband.

'Oh, it would be at least…' begins his Lordship.

'Haha! Never mind what it cost. As Robbo said, what's the point of money if you don't spend it? Right, what about that sing song? Come on everyone, we're wasting valuable time,' Geordie says as he steps on the yellow skin.

'About £550, by perchance?' Jackie asks.

'Yes, I'd say you were in the ballpark,' Stanley replies.

'Well, you lot can sit around here discussing the price of things, but I for one am heading outside,' Geordie says as he makes a dart for the door. Jackie blocks him and takes him by the elbow.

'Geordie, I'd like a quite word, upstairs, if you don't mind,' she whispers. It wasn't a request.

*****

The brazier is roaring, the Christmas lights are twinkling on the tree, snow lays thick all around and the children are sitting comfortably in chairs sipping hot chocolate with marshmallows floating on top. Everyone is ready for the carols but we're still missing two people—Jackie and Geordie.

'Where are they?' I whisper to Fiona.

'They're still in their bedroom.'

'That's nearly twenty minutes. It's getting embarrassing, his Lordship can obviously tell that something is amiss. I'll try and distract him. Okay, everyone,' I shout, 'who wants a glass of warm mulled wine?' There's a cheer from the adults and a tiny "Yes please, Uncle Will" from Katrina.

'You can't have mulled wine,' Wallace informs her.

'Why not?' she pouts.

'Because it's only for grownups.'

'I am grown up. I'll be six next birthday.' I take a head count.

'Stanley, could you spare a hand to help me with the mulled wine?'

'Of course, Will. Delighted to help. Actually, it's one of my specialities.'

'Excellent, you can give me some tips.'

After ten minutes we are back outside with a tray of mulled wine. There's still no sign of Jackie or Geordie.

'You best go get them,' I tell Fiona.

'Don't be daft. They're discussing important matters.'

'Or maybe they're indulging in a quicky while we all freeze our nuts off out here.'

'Rest assured, they will not be engaging in a quicky, that I can guarantee. If they're not here in five, we'll start without them.'

'Speak of the devil, here they come. Okay, everyone, the carols are about to begin. Gather around the tree. Has everyone got their lyric sheets?' Geordie sits behind the keyboard and plays a few scales to test the volume. He's extremely red in the face. I sidle over to him and grab my acoustic guitar as Robbo straps on the acoustic bass and Flaky slips the tom-toms between his knees. 'Everything okay, brother?' I ask.

'Aye. Everything's good,' he says, without emotion.

'All sorted?'

'Aye.' I throw a quick glance over at Jackie who seems to be in buoyant spirits as she chats excitedly to Fiona, Gillian and Julie.

'You sure everything's all right?'

He stares back at me. 'Like I said, everything is sweet. Tomorrow, Jackie and I will be paying a visit to Skipton and a certain little jeweller's shop on the high street. This holiday has cost me a small fortune. It would have been cheaper for me to rent a Caribbean island and employ the Queen's butler to wait on me hand and foot.'

I grin at him. 'Look on the bright side?'

'What bright side?'

'You'll get a discount in the Boxing Day sales.'

'You're a funny man.'

'I try. Right, everyone, after three; one, two, three…'

*****

I close the bedroom door behind me and begin to undress. Fiona sits on the edge of the bed in her pyjamas, rubbing moisturiser into her hands.

'I've checked on the kids. They're all fast asleep—bless them, as are the adults, I think.

'Twas brillig, and the slithy toves, did gyre and gimble in the wabe; all mimsy were the borogoves, and the mome raths outgrabe.'

Fiona giggles. 'Lewis Carroll, Through the Looking Glass. What made you think of the Jabberwocky?'

'It's what Flaky called Geordie yesterday after he'd been slapped on the arse with the blade of a 26-inch Spear and Jackson wood saw,' I say, pulling off my socks and throwing them at the armchair.

'You're worse than the children.'

'Only one of us.'

'It's sad,' she says.

'What is?'

'Stanley, Lord Cumberfutch.'

'Why?'

'He has nobody. He's bereft of family.'

'No, he's not. He has our family now, our extended family. That should be enough for any man.'

She smiles. 'Yes, I suppose you're right.'

'Never suppose I'm right. I'm usually wrong about most things.'

'Have you enjoyed today?'

'Yes, it was brilliant, all things considered.'

She smiles as she brushes her hair. 'I think it's been one of the happiest days of my life. To witness the expressions on the little one's faces as they walked into the living room and saw the presents that Santa had brought them.'

'Yes, that and the expression on Jackie's face when she opened Geordie's present—pure gold.'

'Oh my God! What was he thinking? A box of Milk Tray chocolates and a £50 Sportsgirl voucher. I could tell she was fuming, although she did well to hide it.'

'The eyes?'

'Yes, her eyes seemed to expand. You could almost see the steam coming out of her ears. Especially after all the lovely presents the rest of us received.'

'You don't know the half of it,' I say as I turn my lamp off, clamber into bed, pull the duvet over me and rest my head on the pillow.

'What do you mean?'

'He also had another present I persuaded him not to give her.'

'What was it?'

'An ironing board cover,' I yawn. She stops brushing her hair.

'You've got to be joking!'

'I jest ye not.'

'How does his mind work?'

'Aha, that's the million-dollar question. I don't think it does, not in the conventional sense. It's a riddle wrapped in a mystery placed inside an idiot. When he finally shuffles off this mortal coil, I hope he donates his brain to medical science. It will keep the greatest students of psychiatry puzzled for eons.'

'Has he always been like this?'

117

'Yep. Since the first day I met him. He thrives on chaos, calamity and adversity. He gains some perverse pleasure from it... a natural born agitator.'

'Don't be mean about your best friend. I know he can be foolish sometimes, but he's still loving and adorable.'

'Yeah, like a pet crocodile. I'll give him his dues though; he always pulls through. Every scrape and pickle he gets us into we always emerge on the other side, not totally unscathed, but at least still in one piece. He's a survivor is Geordie.'

'Did he tell you about their discussion?'

'The trip to the jewellers?'

'Yes.'

'What does she want? A ring?'

'Oh, no! She's going the Full Monty; a ring, a necklace and a bracelet.'

'Ouch!'

'Gold and diamonds.'

'Double ouch. Can you draw the curtains, love?'

'No, let's leave them open tonight. The red and orange glow from the Christmas tree lights makes me feel warm and cosy. It's a beautiful tree. Well worth the effort.'

'Easy for you to say.' She flicks her lamp off and climbs into bed, cuddling tightly into me. She lays her arm across my chest and gently tickles my shoulder. 'Have you really enjoyed today?'

'Uh, huh,' I reply as sleep filters through every fibre of my being.

'Is that a yes?'

'Yes.'

'Me and the girls were talking just before bed.'

'That's nice.'

'Everyone has had a fabulous day, even Jackie. She's not too mad with him.'

'That's good.'

'We all agreed that wouldn't it be nice if we made this a family tradition, you know, each year we all gather for Christmas at our place. What do you think?'

'Uh, huh.' Her lips touch my cheek as I become pleasantly woozy.

'Is that a yes?'

'Uh, huh.'

'Good. That's agreed then. Night, sweetheart. I love you.' They're the last words I hear as a blissful heavy darkness wraps me in cotton wool and whisks me away.

Thank You For Reading

I hope you enjoyed this Shooting Star Christmas novella. If you are new to this series then why not go back to the very beginning and read Book 1 "Arc Of A Shooting Star"

If you would like to keep up to date with my book news, there are a few simple ways to be notified.

You can subscribe to my entertaining, monthly "Discombobulated" newsletter. This not only keeps you abreast of new releases, but I sometimes have a free book to giveaway or heavy discounts throughout the year. It's also a good laugh – there's no hard sell – I promise. You can sign up by following the link below which will take you to my website.

I would like to subscribe to your newsletter.

Alternatively, you can go to the following sites and click on the "Follow" button.

BookBub

Amazon

Facebook

For paperback readers, the links above won't work no matter how many times you tap your finger on them. Below is a manual link for my newsletter to type into your browser. For the other sites, Google the site and my name, and it should provide a link.

https://www.subscribepage.com/author_simon_northouse_home

All **reviews** are appreciated.

If you would like to contact me personally, here's my email address.

simon@simonnorthouse.com – I always enjoy a chat and will reply.

About the Author

Simon Northouse is the author of:

The Shooting Star series

The Soul Love series

The School Days series

Let's Get Discombobulated Newsletters

Made in the USA
Coppell, TX
21 December 2020